Praise for the Novels of
LOREN D. ESTLEMAN

BLOODY SEASON

"You won't put this book down."
—Elmer Kelton, author of *The Pumpkin Rollers*

"Estleman's account of events following the O.K. Corral gunfight is the best one I've ever read by far."
—Elmore Leonard, author of *Out of Sight*

JOURNEY OF THE DEAD

"Hard-rubbed dialogue as bright as a new-minted Indian head penny . . . style to burn, talk that haunts. Deserves blue ribbons and rosettes."
—*Kirkus Reviews*

BILLY GASHADE

"Lyrical and alive . . . Rousing and entertaining."
—*Publishers Weekly* (starred review)

CITY OF WIDOWS

"Prose as picturesque as the Painted Desert."
—*The New York Times*

MISTER ST. JOHN

Loren D. Estleman

JOVE BOOKS, NEW YORK

All of the characters in this book are fictitious, and any resemblance to actual persons, living or dead, with the exception of historical personages, is purely coincidental.

MISTER ST. JOHN

A Jove Book / published by arrangement with the author

PRINTING HISTORY
Previously published by Ballantine Books
Jove edition / October 1999

The Penguin Putnam Inc. World Wide Web site address is
http://www.penguinputnam.com

ISBN: 0-515-12657-8

A JOVE BOOK®
Jove Books are published by The Berkley Publishing Group,
a division of Penguin Putnam Inc.,
375 Hudson Street, New York, New York 10014.
JOVE and the "J" design
are trademarks belonging to Penguin Putnam Inc.

PRINTED IN THE UNITED STATES OF AMERICA

10 9 8 7 6 5 4 3 2 1

To my family

MISTER
ST. JOHN

ONE

Bankers' Hours

The first time Mr. Thorson met Donald Quix his faith in the youth of America was restored. In his mid-twenties, on the short side but solid, Quix had pale yellow hair with just the suggestion of a cowlick to soften the effect of his city attire, and was clean-shaven but for a pair of dark burnsides. His boiled shirt was so white it looked blue under the electric lights. He had a warm smile and his grip was firm and dry, two things in which the executive placed much faith. He carried a shiny black leather brief-case.

Once inside the railing that separated Thorson's cubicle from the rest of the bank, Quix identified himself as a local contributor to the *Cheyenne Detective Quarterly* and asked the portly manager if they might discuss the precautions his establishment was taking against robbery for an article Quix was planning on modern law enforcement. When Thorson hesitated, the young man produced a card printed on handsome pebbled stock and invited him to call the number in the lower left-hand corner for confirmation. The manager used his new telephone to speak with a man named Roland A. Rockaway, periodicals editor for Great West Publications, who said, yes, he did employ a writer named

Quix who was researching crime prevention in southern Wyoming, and described him down to his cowlick and burnsides. Thorson thanked him and rang off, all smiles. The home office had been after him for some time to do something about the branch's image.

For half an hour the manager held forth on vault thicknesses, alarm systems, and guard selection while his guest scribbled in a pad taken from the briefcase and interrupted occasionally with a question about schedules and money movements to and from the bank. Afterward Thorson escorted him through the building, introduced him to the second guard inside the vault, and demonstrated the time lock. The journalist was impressed. He thanked his host and left after shaking hands, with a promise to return the next day with a photographer.

A representative from the bank's home office dropped in shortly after closing that evening. Told of the interview, he flew into a rage, accusing Thorson of rank stupidity or criminal collusion or both and threatened an investigation into his personal finances. The manager was surprised and incensed. He took up Quix's card, banged the telephone down in front of the representative, and suggested he find out for himself that the stranger was who he said he was. The call was made, but no one answered. Thorson pointed out that it was after five and that the offices of Great West Publications were no doubt closed. Perhaps, said the other, then rattled the prong and asked the operator to connect him with the sheriff.

When the doors of the bank opened at nine the next morning the man from the home office was inside along with Thorson, the sheriff, and two of his deputies, with two more stationed in front of the building and a fifth in back. Business proceeded as usual until half past ten, when Donald Quix arrived in the company of another young man wearing a U.S. Army knapsack over one shoulder and carrying a camera and tripod. They were stopped at the door and searched, but no arms were found. The knapsack proved to contain photographic plates and a can of flash powder, which the deputies were warned against opening for fear of igniting the contents. This was confiscated unopened. The back was removed from the camera to reveal nothing of dubious nature inside.

Quix was disappointed but cooperative, unlike his companion, who had to be restrained at first lest he strike one of the lawmen and who later proposed to the writer amid much profanity that they withdraw and offer immortality to some other bank. Though the fellow was taller and darker than Quix and wore a moustache, Thorson noticed a definite family resemblance, and supposed the two were brothers.

Despite their innocence of weapons the sheriff was disposed to jail the pair for questioning, but Quix suggested that they try again to reach his editor. Reluctantly the peace officer raised the receiver and asked for the number. For some moments he listened, while observers noted from the whitening of his lips and the snarling from the earpiece that he was getting hard advice from Roland A. Rockaway. He hung up, turned to the man from the home office, and released his pent-up fury in a remarkable display of nonrepetitive obscenity, before which the executive withered. The sheriff left then, with his deputies in tow.

Pale and shaking, the home office representative stammered an apology to the journalists and instructed Thorson to see that they were extended every courtesy. Then he too went out, nearly colliding with a customer coming in, a cripple with no hands. At this the photographer laughed nastily.

For the first shot, Quix wanted all of the bank's employees gathered in front of the open vault with the manager in the middle. The guard on duty in the lobby handed the can of flash powder to the photographer while his counterpart was summoned from the vault's interior. The writer spent some time arranging the tableau, then stood back to inspect his handiwork, bantering gaily to break the ice formed by the journalists' rude reception and the employees' nervousness. At length he nodded to the photographer, who finished adjusting his tripod and tugged the lid off the powder can. From inside he drew a short-barreled handgun, cocking it as he pointed it at Thorson.

There was a short, shocked silence. Then the lobby guard slapped at his side arm. A swift movement nearby checked him. He turned toward the man with no hands to see the muzzle of a large revolver peeping out of his sleeve, fixed somehow to the stump, with a gold coin attached to the end of the exposed trigger. The other stump was poised to strike the coin.

"Smile," said the man who called himself Donald Quix, relieving the two guards of their weapons.

When the time lock finally delivered Thorson and company from the vault into the sheriff's hands, the manager estimated the bank's loss at fourteen thousand. A posse was formed and descriptions of Quix and his companions were relayed by telephone and telegraph to peace officers throughout the state and beyond the borders, but no arrests were made. The telephone number of Great West Publications was traced to a public booth in Cheyenne. Four days after the robbery, both bank guards were dismissed and Thorson was relieved of his duties as manager. He was replaced by a hard-liner from Denver who shot two toes off his left foot eight weeks later while cleaning his revolver in the office. By that time two more banks and a Union Pacific payroll clerk had been robbed in Colorado and Utah. With some variations, the same basic technique was used in all four operations.

TWO

Election Day

Silk streamers littered the lacquered floor of the hotel ballroom, sad gay scraps trodden and forgotten among the squashed cigar butts, empty whiskey bottles, and other debris of human self-indulgence. Silence had crept in like the jungle reclaiming an abandoned city on the heels of the last emigrant, swallowing whole the visitor's echoing footfall and serving as a cruel reminder of what lay at the end of all man's endeavors. Behind a dais draped with red, white, and blue bunting, a placard the size of a barn door foretold VICTORY in foot-high letters over the portrait of a middle-aged man with confident eyes and a brittle smile under a drooping black moustache shot with gray. Under that, like a children's book illustrator's rendition of shrunken Alice, the man himself sat slumped on the edge of the platform with his back against the speaker's stand. His collar was sprung comically, and though he was facing the door he seemed unaware of his visitor's approach. As the gap narrowed he helped himself to a healthy swig from a steel flask in his hand. Whiskey fumes edged the air.

"Mr. St. John?" inquired the visitor.

The seated man glowered up at him. He had a rectangular face, darker and more weathered than it appeared in the portrait, with sharp high cheekbones and an angular jaw beginning to lose definition beneath sagging folds of flesh. His hair was grayer than his moustache and growing thin at the temples. He looked older than his fifty years.

"What time is it?" His voice was rough but his consonants remained unslurred.

The other hesitated, then drew out his watch. "A little before twelve."

"It's still today, then. Amazing. Got something to write with?"

"I think so." Putting away the timepiece, the visitor patted his pockets and came up with a pad and pencil.

"Write that on November 6, 1906, Irons St. John, Democratic candidate for the House of Representatives from the great State of Missouri, got clobbered by a Massachusetts carpetbagger half his age by a vote of three to one. Write how his friends and loyal supporters made a dash for the door when the vote tallies started coming in."

The other wrote. "What do you want done with it when I'm finished?"

"Bury it." The flask gurgled. "Just like they did with that stuff at the St. Louis Fair. Maybe somebody will dig it up a hundred years from now and I'll be famous."

"You're famous now."

"Popular, too. Have some champagne. There's enough there to float a buffalo." He waved an arm toward a table bristling with unopened bottles.

"Could be your friends and supporters don't like self-pity."

St. John looked at him again, his eyes in focus this time. "Man in the Nations died for saying less than that to me." His tone was flat.

"Jack LeFever," said the visitor. "He called you a liar and you blew his belly out his backside with a twelve-gauge shotgun. You were jailed in Fort Smith, but the jury voted for acquittal because LeFever was a known rapist and Judge Parker needed deputy marshals. It was either hang or raise your hand and say 'I do.' "

For a space the ex-candidate studied him without speaking. His visitor was a tall man twenty years his junior, with a bold bent nose and a red beard cropped so close it looked at first glance like a week's worth of neglect. He wore a homburg tilted rakishly over one brown eye and a three-piece suit with a quiet check. No overcoat; it wouldn't be needed in that part of Missouri for another month.

"You're pretty good," St. John said at length. "Even the Republicans didn't find that, and they dug. Anything else, or is that your load?"

"Hardly." The bearded man paged back through his notepad. "You were born in Rockville, Maryland, March 12, 1856, the son of Thomas and Victoria Venable St. John. Your mother died when you were eleven and your father took you to Illinois to live with relatives and returned home. You never saw him again. At the age of sixteen you ran away to Mexico to fight for President Juárez against Díaz and lost. The following year you were seen running with a number of border gangs in Arizona and New Mexico, and you were arrested two years later in Austin for the robbery of the Texas & Pacific Railroad, but the charges were dismissed for lack of evidence. Then came the LeFever killing, and then your service for Parker in the Nations. As a peace officer you're considered in the company of Heck Thomas and Bill Tilghman. As an outlaw, well"—he shrugged, flipping shut the pad.

The primordial silence that had greeted the visitor strained at the rafters. Finally St. John spoke. "Pinkerton, right?"

Nodding, the other traded the pad for a leather folder and displayed his badge and identification. "Emmett Force Rawlings. I'm a field operative based in Cheyenne."

"Wyoming?" St. John's face took on an oriental cast. "Who hired you, my wife? Tell her I'm not coming back till that mother of hers makes an honest effort to drag herself through death's door. I waited eight years and gave up."

"I don't know your wife. My agency has been engaged by the governor of Wyoming to investigate a series of robberies that have taken place there and in the neighboring states recently. I'm sure you've heard of Race Buckner.''

"I haven't heard of anyone or anything since January. I've been sort of busy getting ready to go to Washington.''

"The Union Pacific will pay five thousand dollars for his capture, dead or alive. Two weeks ago he and his gang stuck up a railroad paymaster in Utah for six thousand. We have positive identifications in the other robberies as well.''

"Keep talking, Mr. Force.''

"Rawlings," corrected the Pinkerton. "I've been authorized to engage you to gather a posse for the purpose of running down and apprehending the Buckner gang.''

"Sorry you came all this way." He tipped up the flask.

"Why should you be sorry?''

"I could of said no over the telephone and saved you train fare. I haven't sat a horse in over two years. Besides, I got too many rings around my trunk for all that fool stuff. I gave it up years ago when I went into business.''

"Businesses. Plural. You had three. They all failed.''

"Hell's bells." St. John burped. "Just how far up does your information go?''

The Pinkerton smiled for the first time. "November 6, 1906.''

"What are you offering, Mr. Crawlings?''

"That's Rawlings." He spelled it. "In addition to the railroad's five thousand I'm empowered to offer you another five thousand from the governor for Buckner and a thousand dollars for each of his accomplices. There are at least four. On top of that, the Pinkerton National Detective Agency will pay wages of up to a hundred fifty per week to every man in your posse up to ten, plus six cents a mile. We will also take care of any reasonable expenses.''

"You really want him, don't you?" The former candidate was watching him at eye level now, Rawlings having stooped forward with his hands on his knees. Then the detective straightened.

"It's a new century," he explained. "It's the intention of the governor and my employers to show that there's no longer any place in the West for this kind of banditry. May

I have your answer now, or would you prefer to sleep on it?''

St. John stared toward a pile of discarded placards tacked to sticks for carrying, each bearing his picture. ''Thing like that could run into real money if it goes longer than a couple of weeks.''

''We're prepared to take that chance.''

The older man considered.

''Tell you what, son,'' he said. ''I'll do her for twenty thousand. Flat fee, and I'll pay the wages.''

''I don't have bargaining power.''

''Then get on the horn to your boss. Twenty thousand, success guaranteed. If Buckner's still loose six weeks after I start, you don't owe me a whorehouse token.''

''It's interesting.'' Rawlings felt a slight stirring of distaste now that the other was calling him son. ''You realize that you stand to make far more if the chase drags on.''

''Son, I don't stand to make a cent. I owe seventeen thousand for my campaign, and if I don't pay up by the end of the year I'm out on my ass. I'm too old to start over again with just a saddle.''

''I'll call Cheyenne tomorrow. I feel certain something can be arranged.'' He paused. ''One thing. I'm going along on the manhunt.''

He was expecting an argument, but St. John merely nodded. ''How's your eye? Can you shoot?''

''I was Laramie County champion last year.''

''Ever kill a man?''

''Once, down in Las Guásimas.''

''Like it?''

''Some did. I wasn't among them. Is that a mark against me?''

The old lawman started to wet his throat again, then stopped. He squinted at Rawlings. ''You don't favor me, do you?''

''Let's say I don't favor what you stand for,'' said the other. ''If there's no room out West for the likes of Race Buckner, there's hardly room for you. Your methods are out of fashion.''

"You think that, how come you're here?"

"Two reasons. My employers don't agree with me, and I have bills to pay like everyone else."

St. John grunted. It might have been a chuckle, but he was too far gone in drink for the Pinkerton to tell. "Well, campfire talk will be lively, and that's a fact." He shook the last drops out of the steel container onto his tongue. "I never met a man liked killing I cared to ride with. But caring to and having to don't sprout from the same twig. If I can reach him, you'll be meeting a man who pure-dee loves it. There'll be two others, not counting him. I do the picking. Objections?"

"None." Outside the ballroom a hall clock chimed the hour. "I understand you're registered in Suite 101. We'll meet there this morning at ten and go over the details, if that's all right. By then I should have spoken with my superiors." Rawlings hesitated. "Do you, er, require assistance with the stairs?"

St. John made himself comfortable, detaching his collar the rest of the way and flinging it to the floor. It scrabbled across the glossy surface like a startled crab.

"Won't need stairs. I rented this room for the night and I aim to get my money's worth. You might pass me two or three of those champagne bottles, though. And ask one of the maids to dust me off around nine."

THREE

Cowboys and Indians

"What the hell is *that*?"

George American Horse was seated on a canvas stool before the mirror in his tent, smearing war paint on his round, pockmarked face when a Negro grip came in carrying a long feathered something that at first glance resembled a prostitute's boa. The Indian was a compact five-five with powerful shoulders wormy with thick white scars and long black hair parted in the middle and drawn into twin braids that hung to his naked chest. He wore moccasins and a breech-clout with one nonauthentic feature, a broad leather belt cinched at the waist to hold in his thickening stomach. His shoulders glistened in the Florida heat. He stared at the gaudy construction.

"It suppose to be a warbonnet," said the grip, grinning nervously as he laid it across George's footlocker. "Mr. Tom, he say you's to wear it in the battle today."

George stood and picked up the item. It was a sturdy piece of work, made of bleached eagle feathers tipped black and sewn into soft chamois leather studded with red and blue beads. Strips of ermine hung down on either side of the headpiece and the train was long enough to brush the ground when worn. He dropped it back onto the footlocker.

"No Indian ever wore anything like that," he protested. "Mr. Tom, he say—"

"Tell Comanche Tom that if he really was present at Quanah Parker's surrender as he claims, he'd know that Comanches don't wear warbonnets. Not that kind, anyway. I went along with him on this duel to the death that never took place between him and Parker, but I'm damned if I'll parade around in front of all those people trapped like a New Orleans whore. Tell him that."

"He done said you'd talk like that. He say to tell you you's fired iffen you doesn't wear it." The Negro braced himself for the cloudburst. He was a Pennsylvania native who had never seen an Indian before he joined the extravaganza and was terrified of this blooded Crow. But George's reply was quiet.

"Anything else?"

Here she comes, thought the grip. "Yessir. Mr. Tom, he say you's taking a mite long losing lately. It look like he having too tough a time of it, he say. When he gives you that there flip, you's supposed to stay cotched."

The Indian flushed under his brown skin and war paint, but before he could cut loose, the Negro was gone, brushing past Wild Bill Edwards, who was entering through the flap. George laughed in spite of himself and tried on the headdress. "How do I look?"

"Like a soiled dove I humped once in Waco," said Edwards. Tall and worn for his comparative youth, the sharpshooter was outfitted in black from Stetson to two-inch bootheels, with silver embroidery on his shirtfront and rhinestones winking on his gun belt. Twin pearl-handled Colts rode high on his narrow hips. He was also wearing rimless spectacles, which always came off before he stepped out under the lights of the main tent.

Smiling bitterly, the Crow took off the bonnet and slung it over the folding dressing table. "I think the Great Scout's finally getting senile."

"I heard all about it. Why don't you throw a headlock on him next time you're out there and toss him on his fat ass? Maybe it'll jar his brains back into working order."

"Why don't you shoot his toupee off instead of lighting his cigar?"

"Good question. Anyway, you got more right. Tom pays you less than any of us because you're an Indian and he says you'd just spend it all on whiskey and end up scalping somebody. For that you get to go out there day after day in one town after another and lose to him when anyone with half an eye can see he's no match for you. It can't be easy making him look good."

"I need this job, Bill. There's not a lot of call these days for unemployed redskins. Or half-blind train robbers, comes to that." His voice dropped on the last part. No one on the circuit but George knew Edwards' real name and former occupation. The terms of his parole barred him from exhibition.

The sharpshooter watched "Quanah Parker" apply the finishing touches to his fierce makeup with a tobacco-stained forefinger. "The scourge of the M, K & T and Hanging Judge Parker's best Indian tracker. Who'd of thought we'd end up making faces for the rubes in a traveling show a step and a half ahead of the sheriff, and three months past the end of the season to boot?"

"That's not Tom's fault," said George, scowling into the mirror to gauge the effect. "Breaking even's a dream with *The Great Train Robbery* playing two miles down the road in Seminole. Between the moving pictures and the rodeos these things are burning out fast. I hear even Cody's added a freak show to take up the slack."

"Cody *is* a freak show." Edwards rubbed his eyes under the glasses.

The Indian caught the movement in the mirror. "Hurt?"

"Just a little blurring. It'll clear up by show time."

"Stop around after your act and I'll put tea on them."

"Hell of a note, me having to load my guns with sand to keep from missing them glass balls, just because Tom won't let me wear the cheaters. The only time I get to do any real shooting is when they take the lights off me so I can put 'em on and fire up his stogie. Maybe that's why I don't foul up out there no matter how mad I get at him. Too proud.''

"Great gunfighters don't wear spectacles."

"Comanches don't wear warbonnets either. You going to?"

George grimaced, for real this time. His face looked like a death's-head now, ghastly white with black circles around the eyes and crimson streaks on his cheeks and forehead. "Even bloodthirsty savages have to eat."

The band was warming up in the main tent. George could feel the *brump-brump* of the tubas through his moccasins. Edwards reached for the flap.

"Tom was a lot easier to work for before he took up with that little trick rider from Montana," he said. "She's two months younger than his oldest daughter. Hell, she ain't much bigger than his hand."

"I hear she's a hell of a lot better, though."

Edwards laughed. George's wit was sharpest when provoked. "Well, break a leg. And remember to roll when you take that spill from your horse this time. Saves wear and tear on the shoulder." He bent to duck through the opening, then straightened, leaving the flap open. "I clean forgot. This came for you a little while ago. I caught the kid peeking through a hole in the Arabian harem's tent." He held out a Western Union envelope.

"Open it and read it, will you, Bill? I've got this crap all over my hands."

The sharpshooter tore into it and snorted. "I'll be damned, it's from Ike St. John!"

The trick riders were just finishing their act as George entered the main tent leading his paint and stood between the half-empty bleachers waiting for his eyes to grow accustomed to the electric light. Hopping down from her milk-white Arabian, Comanche Tom's little blonde from Red Lodge curtsied before the small but enthusiastic crowd and swept up a tiny hand in a gauntleted glove to indicate her fellow performers, including a retired gaucho from South America and a family of circus players on hiatus from

Ringling Brothers. Then the music changed and they led
the horses out to make room for the cowboy clown. Stable
hands waited beyond the circle of light to relieve them of
the reins.

"George," greeted the girl sweetly as she approached
him, and the Indian knew he was in trouble, "you speak
Spanish, don't you?"

"A little." He tried to sound nonchalant, but in truth the
nearness of this fleshy twenty-year-old in her brief white
costume with fringe brought the blood rushing to his face.
For once he was grateful for the heavy war paint.

"Would you please explain to this peppergut"—still
speaking sweetly—"that the next time he puts his hands
on my bottom I'm going to geld him right out there in front
of everyone?"

The Crow had to suppress a smile, not so much because
the man in question, decked out in tights and flat black hat
with balls dangling from the brim, was glancing with curious black eyes from one face to the other, but because
she was patting his arm affectionately as she said it. When
George translated—"*desune sus cojones*"—the gaucho
stiffened, paled slightly under his dark complexion, and,
evidently reading confirmation in the girl's complacent
smile, disengaged himself and exited.

She pecked the Crow's cheek, or rather the air nearby,
and declared, "You're a good Indian, George. I don't care
what Tom says."

"Someone taking my name in vain?"

George turned toward the owner of the rich, stage-trained
baritone striding in through the entrance. Thomas Jefferson
Clay was six-three and running to fat in a costume made
from bleached doeskin with fringes as long as a man's arm,
a belt containing his paunch with an ornate buckle fashioned
after the Indian head on the penny. Hennaed locks swept
from under his white Stetson behind his ears to his collar,
fighting the forward pull of a hooking nose and forked
goatee brushed and dyed to perfection. The cold blue eyes
beloved of dime-novel illustrators up North were faded now
but still commanding, though his jowls were anything but

heroic. He had learned to hold his head so that the light bleached out the shadows underneath.

The bantering nature of his opening line was destroyed by its deadpan delivery; Comanche Tom's sense of humor was no greater than his munificence. Throwing her arms around his neck, the girl from Montana stood on tiptoe to kiss him. He pushed her away gently.

"Not now," he said. "Get ready for the stagecoach robbery. Today I'm putting it on right after the battle instead of the Parade of Nations."

She sighed something about loving great men and trotted out, trailing that faint scent of horse and girl that never failed to stir the Indian.

Instead of leaving to take his position on the other side of the tent as George expected, Comanche Tom remained standing next to him, watching the clown attempting to untangle himself from his lasso to the audience's delight. "What happened to the Parade of Nations?" George asked finally.

"King Edward's drunk again." The famous voice was gruff. "You can't do a Parade of Nations with England falling off his horse all the time. Where's the warbonnet?"

Since it was obvious he was holding it in one hand, the Crow almost didn't answer. Then he remembered the Great Scout's almost nonexistent powers of observation and held it up.

"Put it on, for chrissake! I didn't fork over sixty bucks to have you dragging the feathers in the dust and horseshit."

Reluctantly, George tugged on the headpiece. The train tickled his naked back. His paint nickered and shied from the bizarre vision, but he kept a tight hand on the bit chain.

"That's better," said the showman. "The nigger tell you what I want out there?"

"He said I wasn't losing quick enough." George paused. "Listen, Tom—"

"No, you listen." Turning, Tom jabbed a gloved forefinger at the Indian. "Don't think I don't know what you say about me behind my back just because you were root-

ing rumrunners out of the Osage Hills while I was treading
the boards on the East Coast. It's not you these people pay
to see. I'm the only indispensable member of this troupe.
Mission-school Indians I can get by the trainload, so stay
down when I throw you the first time or I'll fire you and
fix it so you never work in another show in this country.''

The other swallowed his bile. ''I'm trying to tell you
about this wire I—''

''Save it. Right now you're going to get up on that horse
I paid for and give my fans their money's worth.'' He spun
on his heel and left the way he had come.

''Be glad to,'' replied George, but by that time he was
talking to himself.

''Ladeeeeeez and gentlemen,'' bellowed the announcer.

The crowd was tense with anticipation. At the close of
the cowboy clown's act a drum roll had started, accompanied by the dousing of all the lights save one, shining
straight down on the bald head of the stout Irishman, a
magnificently moustachioed specimen in full-dress jacket
and puttees stuffed into the tops of knee-high black boots.
After his greeting he paused—six seconds, no more, no
less—while the roll continued. Then:

''Shortly before dawn on June 27, 1874, seven hundred
Comanche braves laid siege to the trading post at Adobe
Walls, Texas. They were led by Quanah Parker, half-breed
son of Chief Peta Nocona and Cynthia Ann Parker, his
kidnaped bride. For three days the battle raged, until
Quanah challenged the beleaguered whites to send forth a
warrior upon whose scalp would rest the fate of everyone
present. That warrior proved to be a nineteen-year-old scout
named Thomas Clay.

''Ladeeeeeez and gentlemen, I give you Comanche
Tom!'' He gestured grandly with his silk hat into the pitch
blackness. The drum roll ended on a crash of cymbals and
a spotlight burst upon the Great Scout in all his frontier
finery, seated astride a fat palomino arrayed in glittering
gold between the bleachers on the far side of the tent. The
glorious sight tore a collective gasp from the audience, then

wild applause and cheering as Tom swept off his big Stetson in the classic pose.

The drum started up again, and the announcer directed the spectators' attention opposite. "And in this corner"—mild tittering at the phrase borrowed from the ring—"Quanah Parker, last hereditary chief of the great Comanche Nation!"

The sudden bright light startled the paint, which squealed and tried to rear as it had many times before. This time George let it. The tableau of the great painted chief in feathers straddling a pawing, whinnying steed was rewarded with thunderous clapping and stamping of feet, louder even than Tom's reception. But barely loud enough, thought the Indian smugly, to cover the sound of the old scout's gnashing teeth. That stunt alone was good for instant unemployment.

The rest of the lights sprang on and the adversaries pranced into the center of the arena newly vacated by the announcer. Following the script, George circled Comanche Tom while the other danced his beast around to keep him in sight. Twice around, building suspense, and then Quanah charged. With an earsplitting whoop he snatched the tomahawk off his belt and swished it at Tom's head, missing his hat by inches as the scout ducked. The rubber blade whistled convincingly and Tom kicked out a long leg that was supposed to brush the Indian's ribs so he could fake a fall. Instead it connected with full force, driving the air from his lungs and unseating him for real. George landed hard on his right shoulder.

True to its training, the paint trotted toward the bleachers and the waiting attendants. Meanwhile Comanche Tom stepped down from the palomino. By this time the Crow had recovered himself enough to stand, though breathing was difficult and his rib cage was on fire. The scout removed his hat with a flourish and scaled it after the departing steed. This was a fairly new addition to the act, quietly incorporated after an embarrassing episode in which the hat had been knocked roughly from his head during the sham battle and his hairpiece had come off with it. At a

distance of eight feet the opponents sank into a crouch and
circled, eyeing each other warily.

"You miscalculated that kick," said George in a low
voice, and feinted with his right hand.

Tom dodged the maneuver. "Want to bet?" He lunged,
grabbing for the Indian. George sprang back.

Here the script called for Quanah to produce a knife and
charge the scout. Tom would lose his balance and fall and
the two would begin wrestling, the wicked-looking blade
inches away from slashing the white man's throat until he
threw the Indian, disarming him and winning the battle.
George reached back for the rubber knife, and while he was
reaching he kicked Comanche Tom as hard as he could in
the groin.

The showman's hoarse cry was heard all over the tent.
He doubled over, only to be straightened out by George's
linked hands scooping up with all the force he could muster
under Tom's chin. It was enough. Fans of the Great Scout
watched openmouthed as their hero tipped over backward
like a great paunchy board and landed spreadeagled in the
dust. The bleachers were silent.

Out of the corner of his eye George glimpsed the rotund
Irishman gesticulating wildly at the band. As the brass
hurled itself into Comanche Tom's victory sting, the Crow
had a sudden inspiration, bent over the fallen scout, and
yanked off his toupee. To the accompaniment of blaring
horns he held up his trophy for all to see, then tossed it
onto Tom's heaving chest, where it clung for a moment
like some large hairy parasite before sliding off.

The laughter deafened him as he thrust the warbonnet
into the hands of the startled Negro grip and left the tent
for the last time.

FOUR

The Lamp of the Wicked

No one hated the Roman Catholic faith more than Midian Pierce, and yet he was inclined to agree with its followers that a house of God should represent His holy majesty on earth. Stranded in a box of a one-room Nebraska schoolhouse that was his only on Sunday afternoons, his nostrils full of chalk dust and cheap varnish and pencil shavings, he envied that Church its vaults and groins and lofty graven altars, its receptacles of blessed water and acres of gold candlesticks. Especially the gold candlesticks. He had stolen one from a church during the Lawrence raid in '63 and, when camped, used to take it out of his saddle-bag and study it by firelight, tracing with callused fingers the lips and whorls cast (or so he fancied) from the heathen wealth of some dead Aztec long after the flames had guttered out. The stick had been taken from him when he was arrested in Hannibal after the war, but he never forgot it, or the opulence of the place from which it had been seized.

But daydreaming was sinful, and he was annoyed to find himself fondling the metal rule on his desk as if it were that long-lost booty. It dropped with a clank, startling fourteen-year-old Becky Howlett out of her contemplation of the *Young People's Book of Bible Stories* open on the

desk in front of her. The teacher's fierce countenance, however, drove her back to her studies. Immediately after her
eyes dropped, so did the stern expression. She was a pretty
blonde with a woman's burgeoning body under the little-
girl gingham, which was the real reason he had asked her
to remain after class.

Midian Pierce was born under a different name sixty-one
years earlier to an unlettered Illinois farmer and his slow-
witted wife, who stood by desperately trying to understand
what was happening whenever her husband took a harness
to the boy for some real or suspected transgression. At
twelve Midian was seduced by his fifth-grade teacher, a tall
woman with a moustache and a bosom like a pillow, and
he left home in a hurry eighteen months later upon learning
that a neighbor was looking for him with a hay knife in
connection with the not entirely one-sided violation of his
sixteen-year-old daughter.

He found employment as a mule driver maintaining the
Illinois and Michigan Canal, which ended when he tired of
the back-bending labor and broke his foreman's jaw. He
used his wages to purchase a plot of land near Springfield,
Missouri, and took a wife, only to find that the work in-
volved in maintaining both a farm and a marriage was
worse than what he had left behind. Shortly after hostilities
broke out between the states in 1861 he left his plow standing in the middle of the field and signed on with the Con-
federacy. He never saw his wife or his land again and
seldom thought of either. When Missouri was occupied by
Union forces he deserted his company and joined the guer-
rillas led by William Clarke Quantrill, with whom he distinguished himself at Lawrence and Centralia as a cool and
efficient killer.

Fortunately for him, Pierce was slight and ordinary of
feature, and after his arrest in Hannibal none of those who
had survived the band's two most notorious raids could
identify him as one of the perpetrators. Instead of hanging,
he was therefore found guilty only of stealing from the
Church and sentenced to serve two years in the state penitentiary at Jefferson City. There he pursued his newfound

interest in religion when a fellow inmate convicted of rape
and murder bequeathed him his Bible shortly before mount-
ing the scaffold.

Three years' study—he served an additional twelve
months for crippling a cellmate who had laughed at his
nightly prayers—fitted him for a career as an itinerant
preacher. From the day of his release to this, with but an
occasional lapse into his former ways and one long period
spent as a professional manhunter with Irons St. John in
the Nations, he had plied his trade with a purpose, depend-
ing upon the generosity of the faithful in return for the
Word. A fundamentalist by necessity, he cared little for
individual denominations save where they suited his convenience. If the community were largely Baptist, then a
Baptist he became; Episcopal, then he reversed his collar
and cursed the Pope; Presbyterian, then he sprinkled his
sermons with quotes from Ecclesiastes and Calvin; and so
on, except for Catholicism, which he despised without
really knowing why; except that it seemed to be expected
of him.

And in every community, he recalled with a prim little
smile as unconsciously he resumed fingering the steel rule,
there had been a Becky Howlett, bright-eyed and fresh-
scrubbed, full of the ecstasy of true devotion. How many
he had blessed! And yet his mission was still so very far
from over. So much to do and so little time.

"Come here, child."

She glanced up hesitantly, perhaps fearful that she had
done something to arouse the instructor's wrath. Often
enough she had witnessed the short, swift arc of the rule,
heard the sharp crack of steel on bone as classroom male-
factors meekly extended their knuckles for punishment. But
she found no reproach in Pierce's expression, and so she
closed her book and got up to obey.

The teacher flattered himself that age had been more than
kind to him, stamping character upon features that in his
youth had been only average and weaving distinguished
gray among auburn locks parted neatly but not severely in
the middle, worn long over the tops of his ears and gathered

into an old-fashioned queue behind his neck. His frame was small but slender, for he was indifferent to food, and his worn black suit fitted him like a sheath the knife for which it was designed. He had brown eyes, a gentle jaw, and the general appearance of a Puritan straight out of the lithographs in the history textbooks used in that same room during the week. Most people were surprised when he told them how old he was.

"Fear not, child," he said, when she stopped six feet short of the desk, hands folded in front of her. "Am I so hideous that you fancy I will devour you?"

"Oh, no!" she blurted. "You're very—pleasing."

"Pleasing." He picked up the rule and dropped it, picked it up and dropped it twice more. "Come closer, child. Shouting is not my way. No, no. Behind the desk."

When she drew near he learned that she was wearing lemon verbena, and scowled. He disapproved of scents. Later he would lecture her on the anointing of corpses. Later, definitely.

Someone battered the door. The girl sprang away, her eyes wide and frightened like a deer's. He got up with an oath and strode down the aisle to the door, tugging down the corners of his vest. The knocking grew insistent.

"Patience, in the Savior's name," he muttered and opened the door on the sheriff.

Now six months into his first term, Fred Dieterle was a hard-eyed oak of a man thirty years old in a buff uniform with a gold star pinned over one leather pocket. He dwarfed the teacher, the crown of his slouch hat brushing the top of the doorway. His gaze swept past Pierce and lighted on the girl.

"Go home, Becky."

Flushing from neck to hairline, she hastened down the aisle, collecting her book on the way. Dieterle stepped aside to let her pass.

"Your jurisdiction hardly extends to this classroom, Sheriff," Pierce said. "I am in charge here." He was bartering words for time, wondering whether it was the girl's parents or another student who had reported him. He had to know who before starting his defense. This had happened before in other communities and he had always managed to talk his way around the local unshod law.

"Not much longer. You're going to jail." Dieterle unhooked a pair of bright steel handcuffs from his belt.

"Am I allowed to ask on what charge?"

"Child molesting, as if you didn't know already."

Pierce was on firm ground now. There was no case. By bursting in when he had rather than waiting ten or fifteen minutes, the fool had spoiled the prosecution's chances. "And may I also ask whose child I'm accused of having molested?"

"Seth Johanson's girl. It happened Friday night, when you went out to his place to tutor her."

"Gerda Johanson!" That cow? He hadn't touched her. "Who claims this?" he demanded.

"Gerda. She says you put your hands all over her. I think you done more. It'll come out at the trial. We ain't hung nobody in this century yet. Let's have your wrists." He rattled the cuffs.

"Those won't be necessary. You'll find innocent men make peaceful prisoners." He took his soft black hat from the peg and put it on, smoothing the brim between thumb and forefinger. "I trust your position can stand the waste of taxpayers' money. Who do you think the jury will believe, a man of God or the fat daughter of an illiterate Swede?"

"That's up to them. Meantime I got deputies phoning your name and description to police departments and sheriffs' offices all over this part of the country. We'll see what folks in the other places you stopped got to say about you."

The teacher held on to his dignity with difficulty. To have lived through so much, only to swing for the wish-dream of a pathetic child! The Scriptures did not deal adequately with the Lord's sense of irony. "I'll just get my Bible." He turned.

Dieterle drew his belt gun and rolled back the hammer with a noise like walnuts cracking. "I'll go with you."

Pierce approached the desk on stiff legs, the revolver at his back. He pulled open the top drawer.

"Hold it!" spat the sheriff. Pierce froze while the other reached past him and plucked the Navy Colt off the leather bound Bible.

"I forgot it was there."

"Uh-huh. Let's just see what else you forgot." He tucked the confiscated weapon under his belt next to the cuffs and picked up the book. First he hefted it, then riffled through the coarse pages, looking for a hollow.

Pierce fired the derringer through his right coat pocket, shattering Dieterle's kneecap and cutting short his career.

The sheriff went down shrieking. He tried to raise his gun, but by that time his assailant had freed the small fire-arm from his pocket and he emptied the second barrel at Dieterle's throat. The heavy slug tore through his vocal cords, brushed his spine, and exploded the blackboard behind him, shards of black slate rattling down like dead leaves.

Dieterle supported himself on one hand, the smashed leg stretched out to one side and his other hand clasping his throat. He was coughing blood. Humming "Nearer, My God to Thee," Pierce picked up the sheriff's Smith & Wesson from the floor and reached for the long-barreled Colt in the sheriff's belt.

"Always keep two guns," Pierce told him, cocking the Colt. "Once they find one, they hardly ever look for another." He placed the muzzle to the wounded man's forehead. Dieterle let out a strangled moan.

The door flew open, whacking against the wall on the other side. A big revolver towed a fair-haired deputy over the threshold. Wide blue eyes like Becky's leapt from the man on the floor to Pierce and back to the man on the floor. His mouth hung open. Dieterle had told him to wait outside; two armed men apprehending a child molester looked silly.

The child molester whirled and fired, the report sounding like an echo to the crash of the door, only louder, deafening in the confines of that room. The bullet slapped the deputy's hand into the doorframe and his gun went cartwheeling.

Pierce pulled the trigger twice more. One shot *thupped* against the curve of the lawman's hat brim, and as he ducked, the second nicked the inside of his right thigh. He was bleeding copiously when the fugitive shoved him aside and ran out.

Dieterle's Winton was parked with the motor running in front of the schoolhouse, looking forlornly like a two-seat buckboard after the horse has run off. The county had bought the automobile for his predecessor a year before, but the old peace officer had preferred his buggy and the machine had stood unused in a local barn until after the election. Pierce's horse was three miles down the road at the boardinghouse where he was staying. Curse him for the sin of pride in his physical fitness! He clambered under the wheel.

Pierce had never driven a motorcar, but once in St. Louis he had ridden in an Oldsmobile during a parade and had watched closely the driver's machinations as they were setting out. Reasoning that all these contraptions were alike, he pushed and pulled levers until the car hiccoughed forward with a jerk that snapped his jaws together. A bullet whanged off the left rear fender just as he pulled away. He loosed lead back at the schoolhouse. The deputy ducked back inside. Thus did a peace officer become the victim of the first automobile theft in Nebraska history.

Steering was easy. Pierce had gone half a mile, however, before he grasped the concept of gears and was able to make speed. Road dust billowed over him, breading the heavy black stuff of his suit and lodging in his nostrils and throat. Judgment was surely at hand when machines such as this ruled the highways.

At first he had no idea where he was going, beyond the boardinghouse stable and more familiar means of transportation. Then something crackled in his breast pocket as he manipulated the car around a gopher hole. He took it out. It was St. John's telegram from Kansas City, Missouri, received yesterday. He had read it and stuck it away, glad those posse days were behind him.

"Mysterious ways, Midian," he reminded himself, over the sputtering of the engine.

FIVE

Old Home Week

Though he had been expecting something of the sort, Emmett Force Rawlings was nonplussed when he opened the door of St. John's hotel suite to an Indian, and a singularly sinister-looking one at that. The round face and flat features, dented all over with smallpox scars, came straight out of photographs taken in enemy camps at the close of bloody cavalry campaigns. His white man's attire of woolen greatcoat and shapeless felt hat pulled low on his forehead served only to make him look more—*foreign* was the word that came inappropriately to mind.

For his part, the Indian betrayed no surprise at finding a stranger in his old superior's quarters. His black eyes were flat and lusterless and he seemed content to stand in the hall gripping a battered Army footlocker rather than request admittance.

"Yes?" inquired the Pinkerton.

"I'll be damned. George!"

St. John, emerging from the bathroom in vest and shirt sleeves, hooted and loped across the floral-print carpet to seize the visitor's free hand. "I was starting to think you weren't coming. How the hell are you? Come in, for chrissake."

Smiling thinly, the Indian entered and set down the suitcase, then nodded at the empty hearth. "Get something burning, will you? It's damn cold traveling across country in an unheated baggage car."

"You're in the wrong century," said the old lawman, kicking a dull gong out of the gray steel radiator next to the door. "Don't tell me they still won't let injuns ride with the gentlefolk."

"People don't change as easy as calendars. Your desk clerk tried to throw me out when I came through the lobby. He failed."

"That son of a bitch. I hope you hit him where it shows." St. John clapped a hand on the newcomer's broad shoulder. It wasn't padded as the Pinkerton had suspected. "George American Horse, meet our meal ticket this trip. Emmett Rawlings is that detective I wired you about."

"That much I figured out." The Indian made no move to shake hands. His eyes slid past Rawlings, and the smile faded. "Hello, Testament."

Midian Pierce, seated in a leather-upholstered armchair next to the fireplace, looked at him over the top of his open Bible and said nothing. Hostility crawled beneath the older man's bland expression. George's greeting had been no more friendly, which brought up the detective's opinion of him. He himself had taken an instant dislike to the zealot the first time he had crossed the threshold earlier in the week. He was "Testament" to St. John too, but to Rawlings he was just one of the breed of dangerous fanatics that had decided him to leave his native West Virginia when he was twenty.

George brightened a shade. "Ike, I brought along someone you may remember. . . . Bill?"

The door opened, admitting a lean, bespectacled man half a head taller than Rawlings in a wrinkled traveling suit too short in the sleeves and a soft gray gambler's hat with a flamboyant brim. He seemed no older than the Pinkerton, but his face was haggard and his broad sad smile looked world-weary. Brown stubble blurred the long line of his jaw. He carried a shiny black valise under one arm.

"Bill." St. John sounded puzzled. He squinted, apparently unwilling to don his own glasses in the others' presence for a better look at the new arrival. Rawlings had already noted his vanity. "The name doesn't match the face."

The tall man removed his spectacles. St. John swore.

"Bill, hell!" he exclaimed. "You're—"

"We called him Wild Bill Edwards in Comanche Tom's show," interrupted George. "If it's all the same to you, we'll just keep on calling him that."

"You in trouble, son?" the old lawman looked concerned.

Still grinning, Edwards put his spectacles back on. The thick lenses magnified his eyes twice over. "None you didn't put me in when you arrested me for that Katy Flyer job back in '89. Old Thunder sent me up to Detroit for twenty to life. They paroled me last year. I'm supposed to still be in Michigan."

"Could of been worse," grunted St. John. "Parker had you set for the morning drop if that clerk died."

The Pinkerton grew restless. "You shot a man in the course of a robbery?"

Before Edwards could reply, St. John snorted. "If he'd meant to, that man would be dead and so would he. Bill— I'll get used to that—Bill was in the habit of shooting clerks' buttons off at twenty paces till they decided to open the safe in the express car. They usually did by about the third button."

"What happened in '89?"

"Damn fool clerk moved," Edwards said.

St. John said, "Bill covered his tracks pretty sweet. If George wasn't along, we never would of found him. This Crow can track a cockroach through a busy anthill."

Rawlings studied the desperado. "You must have been awfully young."

"Celebrated my twentieth birthday behind bars."

"Got paper out on you?" St. John asked. Edwards shrugged. "You'd best lay low just in case. There's four bedrooms here; take your pick. The last campaign worker ducked out Wednesday. I won't say what it cost to feed those greedy sons of bitches.''

George said, "We heard about the election on the way here. It's a damn shame.''

"Yeah.''

"You'd of made a lousy congressman anyway, Cap'n,'' put in Edwards. "First time you got in an argument with a Republican, you'd of plugged him in the belly.''

Laughter rose from the trio, dissipating the bitterness. The old lawman poured out drinks from a cut-glass decanter on the pedestal table. Only Pierce and the Indian declined. The former was deep in Leviticus and George never partook. Edwards put down the valise to accept his glass. Something clanked inside the case when it touched the floor.

"I don't think my superiors will appreciate having a parole violator on their payroll,'' said the Pinkerton.

St. John looked at him coolly. "He's on my payroll, not theirs. Besides, we need a sharpshooter, and you'll go a long way before you find one better than Bill.''

"I want it understood that the Pinkerton's don't indulge in unnecessary killing. It's our policy to bring fugitives in alive whenever possible.''

"Mine too, son. But out there it isn't always possible, and that's when a good eye and a steady hand come in handy.''

"As long as the eye *is* good,'' put in Rawlings pointedly.

Edwards said, "Don't worry about that, Mr. Pinkerton.''

"Rawlings.''

"Whatever.'' He lifted the eyeglasses and let them drop back onto his nose. "With these on I can pick the spots off a ladybug across the road, and I got two more pair sewed in the lining of my riding coat.''

"Speaking of sharpshooters,'' said George, "where's Al Herder? I never knew you to go manhunting without him and that Remington rolling-block he always carried.''

St. John's expression was grim. "Al's dead.''

"Damn!'' Edwards touched his glasses.

"What happened?'' asked the Indian.

"My wire caught up with his widow in Pittsburgh. He was in moving pictures, running cattle for a fellow name of Anderson. Six weeks ago some dumb bastard bet him a week's pay he couldn't jump his roan over a six-rail fence. He couldn't. They buried him with a busted neck."

"Damn," repeated Edwards, more subdued this time.

"Pittsburgh, for God's sake." George sounded angry.

Edwards said, "I had him figured to get shot by somebody's husband."

"Yeah." St. John held up his glass. "Al."

The newcomers echoed the name and drank. Rawlings abstained, contemplating the copper-colored brandy in his tumbler. The old lawman set his down almost full. His companion of the past week realized suddenly that he hadn't seen him drink since Election Day.

"The Lord taketh away and the Lord giveth back," announced St. John, glancing slyly at Pierce and his Good Book. The zealot appeared to take no notice of the deliberate misquote. "Bill, damn glad to have you along, even if you are wanted."

It was almost noon. St. John asked the two late arrivals if they were hungry and learned that neither the Indian, who had spent the last few days traveling with luggage, nor Edwards, who had kept him company, had eaten anything substantial since they left Florida. Immediately he called down to the desk for steak and red wine and whatever green vegetables the hotel had on ice. While they waited he introduced Rawlings formally, and over steaming plates the Pinkerton filled in George and Edwards on their mission.

"Race Buckner," he said, producing a WANTED bulletin printed in Wichita September 18, 1903. The photograph was a studio shot of a young man with a boy's face in celluloid collar and cocked derby, a walking stick resting on one shoulder. "He's twenty-six now, single, no arrests. Officials in Kansas want him for selling bogus shares in the King Ranch in and around Dodge City three years ago."

Edwards handed back the circular. "He's come up some."

"His tactics haven't changed." Rawlings recounted the details of the bank robbery in Wyoming. The two new men chuckled.

"Where was this Buckner seventeen years ago when I needed him?" asked Edwards, chewing.

"Finishing fourth grade, if they got his birthday right." St. John was in good spirits.

"Several bank employees and a railroad clerk have placed him at the scene of four holdups in Wyoming, Colorado, and Utah over the past ten weeks. His take so far totals more than thirty-five thousand dollars."

A respectful silence settled over the table, disturbed only by the clicking of Pierce's knife and fork against his plate. He continued to ignore the conversation while eating.

"How many in the gang?" George asked finally.

"Four," replied the Pinkerton. "Counting the man who answers the telephone."

"Five."

All eyes turned to the preacher, busy sawing off a piece of steak the size of his thumbnail. "Why five?" Rawlings inquired patiently.

"Because that's how I'd do it. You said this Buckner was smart."

"I'd listen to him," advised St. John over his wine glass. "Testament thinks like a bandit."

The detective waited, but Pierce made no attempt to clarify. At length Rawlings asked for an explanation. The man's smug indifference was infuriating.

Pierce spoke between bites. "One to watch the people in the bank, one to fill the sack, one at the door, and one to hold the horses. Telephone man makes five."

Rawlings nodded. "All right, we'll say five. Now, as to the other men in the bank. We have a reader on Merle Buckner, Race's first cousin, whose description fits the man posing as the photographer. Thirty, divorced, medium height, dark hair, moustache. He served four years in the Montana State Penitentiary for armed robbery. Ordinarily, because of his age and experience we'd consider him the leader, but since his cousin does all the talking and the method they're using suits him more than Merle, we're assuming otherwise.''

''Like with Jesse and Frank,'' suggested Edwards.

Rawlings ignored the comment. ''We believe their system of getting away employs fresh horses stashed along their escape route in relays, Pony Express style. That refinement we attribute to the Montana branch of the family.''

''What about the man with no hands?'' put in St. John.

''James Blaine Shirley. We think,'' Rawlings added.

Edwards said, ''I've heard that name.''

''No reason you shouldn't have. Besides Roosevelt and Dewey, the Spanish war produced only one national hero, when Shirley threw aside his commanding officer during the siege of Santiago to save him from an explosive device hurled at his feet. He was attempting to toss it clear when it detonated in his hands. Congress awarded him the Medal of Honor. The Wyoming bank manager identified him positively from a newspaper sketch, but witnesses to the other three robberies were less sure.''

The Indian pushed aside his plate and set fire to a long black cheroot that smelled unpleasantly like burning rubber. ''Just how does a man with no hands go about sticking up a bank?''

''Simply and ingeniously.'' The detective held up a bony wrist. ''He wears a double-action Colt strapped to one stump with the butt removed, the trigger guard filed off, and a ten-dollar gold piece welded to the trigger. All he has to do is point the stump and''—he swept his other arm club-fashion back under the extended limb.

''Ha!'' Edwards was delighted. ''But what makes a war hero turn outlaw?''

''You can't eat medals,'' said St. John. To Rawlings: ''What about gunplay?''

''They haven't resorted to it so far.''

''What's this job pay?'' George asked.

''That's my department.'' Removing his napkin from under his chin, the old lawman cleared a space around him. Clutter seemed to inhibit his powers of discussion. ''Two hundred a week, payable at the end of the trail. Pinkertons supply the horses and equipment.''

George said, ''Well, it sure beats Comanche Tom's show. Count me in.''

''Me too,'' said Edwards.

''Testament?'' St. John looked across the table at Pierce, who had finished eating and was sitting back with his eyes closed and his fingers laced across his spare middle. He looked like a thin sinister Buddha.

''I'm here, aren't I?'' he replied.

''Fine. Now we wait.''

''Wait for what?'' Rawlings asked the old lawman.

''Trail's cold. Till they kick a hole in another bank or something, we got no place to go. When they do, we'll be on them like ugly on a buzzard.''

''What if they don't?''

St. John smiled behind his moustache. ''Then I reckon you won't be needing us.''

SIX

Trains

Engineer C. T. Goddard considered the water stop at Elephant Crossing in Colorado the most dangerous and stimulating on the entire weekly Wichita-to-Denver run. Three of his predecessors had looked down the muzzles of guns in the hands of hard-eyed men with bandanas hiked up over their noses on that spot, and he himself had been waylaid there twice. The first time, he had scalded a robber beyond recognition with a jet of steam and made good his escape; on the next attempt he had drawn the bulldog pistol he carried in his hip pocket, killed one bandit, and ran off the rest. No one had bothered him since. E. H. Harriman himself had once remarked that one Goddard was worth twenty armed guards from Wells Fargo.

White head stuck outside the cab, he backed the engine under the spout, where the fireman swung it down to fill the boiler. After twenty-two years with the U.P., Goddard had yet to come to a stop squarely underneath. Sixty yards off the crossing, a cluster of tar paper shacks hunkered sullenly against a red-topped butte that from a distance looked like a gigantic silo, apart from the shacks the only irregularity in hundreds of miles of grassy plain. The settlement had been an end-of-track town that had refused to die when the rails left it behind, preferring to dig in and weather down like a determined scorpion on a bare rock. It had survived—barely—but the effort had sapped all the hospitality from the town, and it was worth a passenger's life to step into the saloon for a quick drink while the train took on water.

Goddard was put on his guard, therefore, when three men in new Stetsons and greatcoats appeared outside the cab as he whooshed to a stop. Two of them wore their coats unbuttoned, a bad sign. The third had his hands in his pockets. The engineer reached behind him, closing his fingers around the butt of the stubby pistol.

"Afternoon." The speaker was young, with light eyebrows and dark burnsides; no whiskers. His voice was pleasant.

Goddard studied their faces. The tallest of the three wore a thick moustache and a grim look. He was older than his companions. The other one, the one with the cold hands, was an inch shorter, with a broad face and his hat down to his eyebrows. An icy breeze came up and lifted his coat collar. He ignored it.

"What do you want?"

The spokesman opened his coat, revealing a Remington on his left hip and a brass star pinned to his shirt. "We're deputy U.S. marshals. We got a wire that a killer escaped from the Kansas State Penitentiary at Lansing six days ago and we think he might be riding your train. Wonder if we might have a look."

"Anyone can lay hold of a badge," said Goddard. "You got a warrant?"

"John Doe." He reached for his breast pocket. The engineer whipped out the bulldog.

"Slow."

Grinning, the stranger unbuttoned the pocket and produced an official-looking document. Goddard read it swiftly, one eye on the trio. Wordlessly he handed it back and put away the gun.

The conductor came hobbling along the cinder bed. He was a small, dark German who had been complaining about his bad feet for as long as the engineer had known him. His blue uniform was dusty, the trousers bagging like rubber waders from his suspenders. "What goes on?" he demanded. "How much water do you need to go forty miles?" Then he noticed the deputies and stopped.

When Goddard filled him in, his narrow face screwed up with annoyance or pain, the engineer couldn't tell which. "How long is this going to take? We have a schedule to maintain." The German addressed himself to the man with the moustache. Of all of them he looked best suited for command. But it was the original deputy who answered.

"Long as it takes to find out if he's on board." He jerked his chin toward the line of cars. There were seven, including the express box and caboose. He and the man with the moustache mounted the first coach, accompanied by the conductor. The third man remained behind with Goddard.

"How's Dan McCoy these days?" the engineer asked.

"Depends on who's Dan McCoy," replied the deputy. He had murky brown eyes that reflected no light.

"Funny you don't know him. He's the marshal hereabouts. Your boss." And Goddard went for the gun in his hip pocket.

With a swift, snakelike maneuver, the other drew his hands out of the pockets of his coat, only he had no hands. In place of his right, the sightless barrel of a Colt extended from the sleeve to within an inch of Goddard's left eye. The other stump crossed underneath. "Stand still or be scraped off the boiler. Your choice."

The engineer obeyed, smiling. "You forgot the fireman," he taunted. "First thing I check after reading my orders is that whoever I ride with is armed. Right now there's a Smith & Wesson forty-four aimed at your head."

"You mean this one?"

The new voice startled Goddard. He half turned and saw the man with the moustache standing in the cab, displaying the big American revolver the fireman always wore under his belt. Of the latter there was no sign. Cold lay like iron against the engineer's back. "Where's Lewis?"

"If you mean the wood monkey, he's taking a little nap.

If you don't want to join him you'd best hand me that jug pecker.'' He reached down a palm. Goddard hesitated, then plucked out the bulldog between thumb and forefinger and laid it in his hand.

"No one's ever robbed a train of mine," he said.

The handless man smiled thinly. "It's a new century, Dad. Lots of things being done that ain't never been done before." He moved the gun a tenth of an inch. "Let's climb up and enjoy the view."

After passing through the coaches and studying dozens of upturned, curious faces, pausing occasionally to question a passenger and scrutinize his identification, the fair deputy asked the conductor to let him into the express car.

"This I cannot do," protested the official, indicating the legend AUTHORIZED PERSONNEL ONLY stenciled on the door.

"Well, if a deputy marshal ain't authorized, who is?"

The German's brow puckered. The other bore in.

"Listen," he said, dropping his lawman's tone. "You got a boss, I got a boss. You know how it is. I go back to the marshal, tell him we didn't find this outlaw, he asks did I search the whole train. I say, 'Yeah, everything but the express car.' He says, 'What's the matter, you scared of the dark?' and I'm back out punching cows. It'll only take a minute."

The conductor sighed, nodded, and rapped on the door. There was a pause, and then a tiny square panel was slid open at eye level. Hostile gray eyes shifted from one face to the other.

"Yeah."

The deputy explained his mission. "Let me just step in-side," he concluded, when the owner of the eyes started to refuse. "Just so I can tell the marshal I looked."

After another short silence the peephole clacked shut and something rattled. The door opened, revealing a paunchy man attired in Wells Fargo's new charcoal-gray uniform with the flap unbuttoned over his side arm. He moved aside to admit the pair. "Make it quick."

The car was a windowless box equipped with a hard

wooden chair apiece for the guard and the clerk—a stout, fiftyish man whose salt-and-pepper whiskers matched his rumpled suit—a table between them upon which rested a deck of cards and two hands of poker laid face down, and a large black iron safe bearing the WELLS, FARGO & CO. logo painted in gilt letters across the front. Once inside, the conductor limped over to the one vacant chair and dropped down with a loud grunt of relief.

"Satisfied?" said the guard to the deputy, who stood just inside the door glancing around. " 'Lessen you figure he's little enough to fit in the safe."

The clerk snorted. Even the conductor snickered in a distracted way, massaging one throbbing foot through the thick oxford. The deputy joined in good-naturedly.

"Open it up," he said, still laughing.

The guard's cynical chuckle rose to a guffaw. The others laughed too, except for the deputy. Then they all fell silent, contemplating the gun in the young man's freckled hand.

"Hold it."

Long-nosed and furtive in a black cutaway, the photographer resembled a six-foot crow crouched behind the camera and tripod, one spindly arm holding up a flashpan heaped high with magnesium powder. He drew a shallow breath, held it, and squeezed the bulb in his other hand. The coach swelled with blinding blue-white light, bleaching out shadows and trapping the grim faces of the men seated on both sides of the aisle, for schoolboys and antiquarians to study fifty years hence and wonder what demons drove the tense bodies strung with iron and leaning on Winchester rifles among the cigar burns on the leather seats. Then the light retreated and black, acrid smoke rolled through the coach.

"History is grateful, gentlemen," announced the photographer, folding his tripod. He was gone before the air cleared.

George American Horse wrenched open his window to breathe and watched Wild Bill Edwards, who had excused himself from the historic sitting, supervising the loading of their horses into the livestock car behind the coach. The animals were all short-coupled and thick of haunch, all in solid duns and grays without a paint or an appaloosa among them. In that respect, he mused, St. John hadn't changed; mottled coats signified too many bloodlines for his trust.

But in other ways the posse chief was a stranger. True, he showed his age, but his character had altered in ways that years alone couldn't explain. Where, for instance, was that nervous energy that used to spark from him like telegraph signals, so that even when he tried to sit still his drumming fingers and tapping toe gave him away? The St. John he knew would have been on his feet that instant after the shutter was released, barking instructions to the train crew, taking charge of every detail of their departure, not trusting the smallest task to anyone but himself. This St. John, relaxing in the seat in front of him and watching the smoke curl up from the end of today's cigar as if it might wander in the wrong direction, would take some getting used to, as did the near-teetotaling St. John he had met in the hotel and the failed politician who had laughed tolerantly at Edwards' crude joke about his loss. Judge Parker's deputy would have knocked Wild Bill across the room. Perhaps his many disappointments had mellowed him, forced upon him the role of philosopher. Or perhaps, the Indian concluded with a sigh, it was he, George, who had changed.

Pierce remained the same, worse luck. Immersed as ever in his prop Bible across the aisle from George, the old hypocrite looked as saintly as he had that day in '96 when they parted company for the last time after bringing in that three-quarter-breed rapist from what was left of the Cherokee Strip. Soon after, Congress disbanded the Fort Smith court and, as if that were the final blow, the Judge himself died, bringing to an end the most remarkable chapter in the history of the frontier. For twenty-one years the stern Ohio Methodist had sat in judgment over seventy thousand square miles of Indian territory—fourteen of those years with no appeal between himself and God Almighty—trying in the process 13,490 defendants and hanging seventy-nine. Many of whom, thought George, were no worse than the

man seated across from him peacefully committing the
Scriptures to memory.

His own distaste for Testament stemmed not from the
glee with which he took human life, or even from his pref-
erence for virgins aged eleven to sixteen (a far greater crime
in those parts), but from a purely personal hatred. Pierce
believed—and it was not an unpopular delusion—that Indians were descended from that lost tribe branded by God
with the mark of Cain and driven from Israel and as such
deserved extinction. The Crow had met his share of redskin
haters, but none held such frightening, fanatical faith in the
righteousness of his prejudice. Zealots of Pierce's stripe
were capable of carrying such a conviction to its fatal ex-
treme at any time without warning, and from what little
George had seen of him since their reunion, he suspected
that his beliefs were unchanged. Fainter, maybe, and not so
likely to erupt into violence without provocation, but there,
lurking beneath the pious facade like rats behind the wain-
scoting. The Indian had never slept soundly in a camp that
contained Midian Pierce.

The posse had grown by two since yesterday. Paco and
Diego Menéndez, sitting behind Pierce, leaned morosely on
their repeaters and took turns staring out their window with
hostile dark eyes. The brothers—if they were brothers; St.
John could get through to them with his Spanish but de-
ciphering their Yaqui-and-Mexican dialect was difficult—
had ridden in the night before looking for a place with the
group. Paco was whipsaw-lean, with a black moustache de-
scribing an inverted V over the corners of his mouth and
matching scars from ears to chin. His taller, bulkier companion had bowlegs and combed his blue-black hair straight
back from forehead to collar. All anyone knew about them
was that they used to ride with a cattle rustler named Villa
below the border. St. John felt they might be useful at one
quarter the wages he was paying the others. They spoke
very little even between themselves, but the Indian suspected that they understood more English than they let on.
He didn't trust them any more than he did Pierce.

Of Rawlings, now perched on the edge of the seat opposite St. John, rummaging through a large open satchel balanced on his knees, George could make little. Like most Pinkertons he was tense and disapproving of his companions, but since he spoke of nothing beyond their mission and kept most of his opinions to himself, his true character remained elusive. That would change, George knew. If you want to learn everything about a man that's worth knowing, camp with him.

Rawlings had traded his city clothes for denims and canvas, topped off by a sombrerolike hat with a tall crown and a broad flat brim, and appeared to be inspecting the contents of his bag to make sure nothing had been forgotten. One of the items thus scrutinized was a portable Kodak camera not much larger than a collar box, considerably more compact and less complicated than the photographer's cumbersome version.

"Illustrating a book, Mr. Rawlings?" asked St. John.

The detective glanced up at his inquisitor, then rewrapped the piece of equipment in a black cloth and returned it to the satchel. "I hope it won't be needed," he said. "I'm required to take pictures of slain fugitives to be checked against Bertillon measurements in Washington for identification from the records. No living person has ever been photographed by this camera."

"We'll try to see you don't use it," said St. John. "But don't count on it."

Rawlings glanced uneasily at the others. "May we speak in private?"

"Sure thing." St. John got up and led the way past George to the rear platform of the car.

The air between the coach and the livestock car where the horses could be heard shuffling and snorting was cold and moist. A mildew-colored sky cast its shadow over the railroad yard and made a dirty smudge of the Kansas City skyline. Even the Missouri River looked motionless and dull. Brown smoke grew crookedly out of factory stacks on the Kansas side. *A good day to cut your throat*, Rawlings' coal-mining father used to say.

"I recognize that you're in charge of this expedition,"

said the Pinkerton, leaning his hands on the platform railing. "But as far as the agency is concerned, I'm responsible for its outcome."

"Sounds about right." St. John puffed his cigar and watched the yard gang greasing the journal boxes. He was wearing an old-style cavalry campaign hat and a hip-length corduroy coat with a bearskin collar. Both had seen much use but now stank of mothballs.

Rawlings continued. "The Union Pacific feels no qualms about bountying the Buckner gang dead or alive. Pinkerton does. If we bring in a wagonload of corpses, I'll have failed in my duty as surely as if we came in empty-handed."

"Get to the point, son."

"To begin with, it strikes me I'm the only member of this posse who doesn't have a criminal record."

The old lawman shifted his weight to look at him. In his trail clothes he looked younger and more rugged than he had at the hotel. "In the first place," he said, "you're wrong. George never did a day in jail. In the second place, none of us are killers, except for Testament. I can't say about the Mexicans. Just having killed doesn't make you a killer. And you'll go a long way out here before you find a man you can count on who hasn't had paper out on him someplace. You knew my past and you still came looking to hire me. I didn't ask you for this job."

"That's not my—" Rawlings began, but was cut off.

"I said already we'd try to bring them in upright and breathing. But you got to understand that doesn't amount to much when it comes down to us or them. They just stuck up a train in 'Rado for twenty thousand in cash and securities. They didn't shoot anyone, but it's sure they would of if something went wrong or a blooded engineer and an armed guard wouldn't of stood by and let them. When we meet up with them, that's what I want you thinking about, and not what your boss will say when you dump a load of dead meat on his doorstep."

The Pinkerton grimaced. "What about Pierce? You say he's a killer. Can he be controlled?"

"He isn't a dog," said the other, with exaggerated patience. "I brought him in because he knows how these people think and because when the time comes to kill he'll do it without having to think about it. Morals are a fine thing, Mr. Rawlings, but sometimes they get the wrong people killed."

"That leaves the Mexicans. What do we know about them?"

"They know their way around guns. With some men you can tell that by looking at them. That's all I need to know right now. If they give us trouble later, we can always shoot them."

The detective looked at him, wondering if he was joking. No smile greeted him. "I hope I haven't made a mistake," he said, after a long moment.

The locomotive whistle blew, a hoarse stridency that set the platform buzzing. St. John clapped a hand on Rawlings' shoulder.

"One thing's sure," he announced. "Good things and mistakes are done when they're done and there's no changing them. Come on inside. You'll like the scenery betwixt here and Elephant Crossing."

The 6 P.M. from Lincoln to Kansas City chattered over the rails at a steady forty miles per hour, its lighted windows painting a yellow streak through the night. In the third coach the conductor handed back the last passenger's ticket and paused near a black porter carrying a cuspidor with his hand inside to avoid smearing the gleaming finish.

"See that fellow in back?" he asked the porter.

The Negro looked at the big man in the last seat, glaring sullenly at the inky blackness outside his window. He was young, but his eyes were hard and his face looked pale and drawn. A kerchief tied around his neck couldn't conceal a startling splash of white at the throat. On the seat in front of him was hooked a stout cane with a rubber tip. "You means the man with the bandage?"

"That's him. Got a stiff leg to boot. How you figure he came by an ugly wound like that?"

"Why don't you ask him?"

"Don't be stupid," said the conductor. "Besides, I don't think he can talk. You know what I think? I think he's an outlaw."

"Maybe a lawman."

"Same thing. Looks like the devil's chasing him, don't he?"

"Or like he chasing the devil." The porter touched his hat and returned to his errand.

For a while the conductor watched the mysterious passenger. Then he gave up and went forward, leaving ex-Sheriff Fred Dieterle to the demons he saw lurking outside.

SEVEN

Stolen Hours

While Irons St. John and company were steaming toward Colorado, their quarry was crossing a snow-covered basin five miles south of Pinto Creek, Wyoming. Chins huddled into their chests so that their hat brims met their standing collars, the four slouched along astride lathered mounts whose breath steamed in the crisp air, casting a smoky haze over the scene that reduced the riders to figures in a faded tintype.

The man in front bore little resemblance to the jaunty youth pictured on Rawlings' dated bulletin. Two days' rusty stubble and a bad sunburn aged him ten years instead of three, and the eyes that glared red-rimmed and watering out of the shadow of his bent-down brim had neither the arrogant directness of the eyes in the photograph nor the earnest, trustworthy look that haunted the nightmares of such as former Bank Manager Thorson and Engineer C. T. Goddard. He rode, as was his habit, with one gloved hand on the reins and the other resting on his left thigh, leaving most of the work to the horse. All he had to do to display his cowboy training was step into leather.

The old man watching them from the door of the exhausted soddy slid his binoculars along the single-file pro-

cession, taking in the older, tense man riding behind the
young leader; the cripple with his reins wrapped around one
stump; the Cherokee woman bringing up the rear in white
man's clothes, her face pumpkin-shaped and oriental under
the ruins of a felt hat dragged down over her long hair.
Behind them the broken teeth of the Laramie Mountains
gnawed at a dull steel sky.

When they were still outside rifle range the group halted.
The man in front stood in his stirrups, his eyes moving past
the building and the five horses in the corral and combing
the terrain beyond. At length he drew his hip gun and fired
a shot into the air. The old man saw the smoke before he
heard the report, warped by wind and distance and echoing
lispingly off the mountains that ringed the basin. In response he hoisted his Springfield rifle and sent a bullet
through the overcast. The blast deafened him momentarily,
as if his ears had been boxed.

Someone let out a whoop and the riders charged the
cabin. The horses put up only a token protest, for they had
caught the welcome scent of woodsmoke. Tiny arcs of
snow flew off their hoofs.

"You're late," observed the old man, as they dismounted before the door.

Merle Buckner snorted. His moustache was ragged and
the ends were frosted white, making him look like a con-
temporary. "A hunnert and fifty miles ain't a walk around
the house. You ought to try her sometime, get rid of that
gut." He poked the other's hard belly, spilling out through
the aperture left by his coat's being buttoned only at the
neck.

"Done her a thousand times," the old man retorted.
"And I had this gut when you was still on ma's milk."

"That'd be about last year, wouldn't it, Merle?" Race
Buckner laughed and stamped snow off his boots before
entering the hut.

While the Indian woman saw to the horses, the others
gathered around a shaky wooden table inside. A fire burned
fitfully in the stone fireplace, spitting inadequate yellow
light now here, now there, making shadows crawl on the

bug-infested walls. Merle opened his coat and unstrapped a canvas money belt from around his middle. He grunted in relief as he flung it down on the table. "Damn thing's been gnawing holes in my hide for a hunnert miles. I should get a bigger cut just for carrying it."

"You volunteered," Race said, opening the compartments and pulling out fistfulls of bills. "You wasn't family, I'd of thought you was fixing to head south."

"I like the feel of it. Or I did." He unbuttoned his shirt to examine the sores in his flesh.

"Any shooting?" The old man stared transfixedly at the cash coming out, his pale tongue moving from side to side in his stubbly white beard.

Merle shook his head. "Like opening sardines. I thought you said that engineer was hard."

"He was back in '97, when Ted Northrup's bunch tried to take that Army payroll. Put Ted's little brother in the ground like he was a carrot seed. Ted never was the same after. They hung him in Texas after he robbed a general store and kilt the clerk. A general store, for chrissake! Frank and Jesse would of kicked his ass."

"Carroll, you do stretch a man's tolerance," said Merle, doing his shirt back up. "The James boys, the Daltons, Butch Cassidy—ain't there anyone famous you didn't ride with?"

"William Bonney. Me and Billy never did work the same place at the same time, though we did share a bottle once in Roswell." He chuckled, ending on a phlegmy cough. "He had the ugliest whore I ever—"

"Shut up while Race is counting."

Carroll swallowed his retort. Jim Shirley, the double amputee, was watching the younger Buckner's hands separating the crumpled bills and notes into piles for enumerating. He seldom spoke. The gang had from time to time included transients who drifted in, rode with them for a while, then drifted out, carrying away the belief that he was mute as well as crippled. Silent, armed men had always unnerved Carroll, and on those rare occasions when this fellow whose revolver was attached to one stump gave voice to a command, the old bandit tended to obey.

"Eight thousand, seven hundred sixty cash," announced Race, smoothing out the last twenty and laying it atop the finished stack.

"What's those?" Carroll pointed a crooked arthritic finger at the heap of neglected notes.

"Bearer bonds," said Merle. "You hand them to the cashier and he gives you money back. You don't have to sign nothing nor show identification. There's eleven thousand dollars' worth there. Counted 'em myself when I put them in the belt."

"Burn them."

All eyes turned to Race. He wasn't smiling. Merle's jaw dropped. "They're good, I said! I unloaded a thousand bucks' worth in Montana before they picked me up."

"Could be that's why they picked you up." His cousin spoke quietly. "They draw too much fire. Folks look too close at your face. You want to do the honors, Carroll?" He shoved the pile toward the old man, who grinned, showing tobacco-stained teeth with many gaps.

"I sure as hell would! Make me feel like Vanderbilt." He scooped up the notes.

"It's like burning money!" Merle moved to stop him.

Race laid a firm hand on his cousin's wrist. "There's no leaders here," Race said. "I vote we play safe and burn the paper. Who votes with me?"

"I vote we don't," spoke up Shirley, after a moment. "Folks stare at me anyway."

"Carroll?" Race looked at the old man.

He rubbed a fistful of notes over his beard. "I may be crazy, but I wouldn't last six months behind no bars," he said. "Let's set fire to it."

"Appears we're tied," observed Merle.

Race said, "The squaw ain't voted."

"Injuns and women don't vote!" Carroll was indignant.

"She gets an equal cut for holding the horses. That entitles her."

"She votes with me," said Shirley.

Race studied him. "She ain't even in the room."

"She votes with me anyway."

Merle was smug. "Well, I reckon that's that. Divvy her up, Carroll. Twenty-two hunnert apiece."

"Horses!" His cousin closed a hand on that butt of the gun in his holster.

The others started, looking around. The hut had no windows.

"I didn't hear nothing." But Merle drew his Remington. Every man in the group carried the same make, except Shirley; it was a Buckner family custom that in Race had become an obsession.

Carroll, who wasn't wearing his, dropped the bonds he was holding and snatched the Springfield out of its corner. He tore aside the buffalo robe he had dropped down over the door after everyone had entered. Merle and Shirley pressed in close beside him. Only Race hung back.

"There ain't—" began Merle, then fell silent. He swung around.

Race was standing empty-handed in front of the fireplace. The flames burned brightly, flicking long yellow fingers up the chimney. Merle's eyes flew to the table. The bearer bonds were gone. "You son of a bitch!" He vaulted toward the hearth. Race stepped in front of it. Halting, his cousin raised his weapon. He was quivering with rage.

"Move aside."

The other shook his head. "Reckon you'll have to shoot, Merle. I done it for us all."

"Put it away," Shirley said quietly.

Merle turned just far enough to include the cripple in his field of vision. Recognizing the crossed-stumps stance, he rammed the Remington into its holster hard enough to pop a stitch on the belt. His face was as white as a clenched knuckle. Suddenly he spun and pushed his way out past the buffalo robe.

"Let him be," advised Race, when Carroll turned to follow him. "He'll be back when he's ready. Just like when he was little."

"Thought you said they wasn't no leaders here." Heavy

shouldered and coated to the knees, Carroll looked like a large gray bear. The rifle dangled at the end of his arm.

"Didn't like the way the vote went." Race took up a crooked stick leaning next to the fireplace and broke up the ashes. A charred corner of paper bearing the inscription FIVE HUNDRED DOLLARS ($500) floated out and drifted unnoticed to the earthen floor.

The air was growing warm. The old man put away his rifle and started wriggling out of his overcoat. "Want help with yours?" he asked Shirley.

"Woman'll do it."

A few minutes later, the squaw called Woman Watching came in carrying two blanket rolls under each arm and dumped them against the wall next to the doorway. Her black eyes glittered from slits in her round, smooth face like those of a fat little boy. She was just twenty. Her pudgy fingers unfastened the buttons on Shirley's coat with a mother's swift efficiency, and when she had freed his stumps from the turned-back sleeves she folded the threadbare garment and hung it over the back of a wooden chair reverently as if it were a gentleman's new ulster. Then she commenced to loosen the straps that anchored the modified Colt to his truncated limb.

"Where'd he get her, anyways?" Carroll whispered to Race. With a rag wrapped around one hand he had lifted a chipped enamel coffee pot from its station in front of the hearth and was filling the second of two tin cups on the table.

The younger Buckner was slouched in the only other chair, both legs stretched out toward the fire. His cup steamed on the table before him, daring him to pick it up. "Jim won't say. He had her when I met him. I heard he bought her off a tinhorn in Oklahoma, but you can't prove it by me. They appear to get on."

"You reckon them two ever—?" The old man looked genuinely curious.

"I don't know," the other said irritably. "Why don't you ask him?"

"Think he'd mind?"

Race looked at him, at his eager, ravaged face, and laughed quietly. The squaw, massaging Shirley's shooting arm through his shirtsleeve where he sat in the chair that supported his coat, shot them a curious glance. "Uncle Carroll," said Race, "you are a one."

"I don't know what you're gabbing about. And quit calling me Uncle."

"It was good enough when Merle and me was kids."

"Well, you ain't kids no more. Just 'cause I knowed your pa don't make us blood relations."

Race sipped carefully from his cup. The coffee burned his tongue and scalded the roof of his mouth. But it felt warm and good in his stomach. He worked the stiffness out of his fingers, realizing for the first time how cold he had been. His thighs ached from straddling a horse for two days and his seat was numb. It had been a long time since he left ranch work. "Any visitors while we was gone?" he asked Carroll.

Standing hunched with both hands around his cup, the old man shook his head fiercely, like a bull buffalo besieged by flies. "Gets lonesome as hell out here. I liked hanging around in Cheyenne waiting for the telephone to ring better. At least I got to jaw with folks passing by."

"We won't use that one again for a spell. We was lucky to get out of it what we did. Had it to do over, I wouldn't use it more than twice in a row." He paused. "We pull out in the morning."

"How come? Law on your heels?"

"I don't know, but it's good to think that way. I'm thinking we'll split up for a little, meet in Casper after the first of the year."

"Never figured you to be one to rabbit for no good reason," snarled Carroll.

Race didn't reply. Instead he drew a folded sheet of stiff paper from inside his coat and flipped it open under the other's nose. It was a reward poster containing the Union Pacific's five-thousand-dollar offer for the younger Buckner, dead or alive. The 1903 photograph smiled irrelevantly under the grim legend.

Carroll whistled. "Where'd you get that?"

"It was nailed to a telephone pole outside Cheyenne. I figure they got them posted all over the state." He dropped it atop the money on the table. "Was just me, I might risk it one more time, but I'm like a brand on the butt of everyone with me."

"How much we got now?"

"Counting this, about forty thousand. That's eight thousand apiece. Any man can sail through all that 'twixt now and the end of the year is a sinful spendthrift."

"It'd make one hell of a stake for something really big."

Something in Carroll's tone drew a thoughtful glance from Race. Then he tilted his hat brim forward over his eyes. "Don't try to tempt me, old man," he said. "Your job's to get a good price for those worn-out horses after we leave. Nobody elected you ramrod."

"Who was the one told you about the banks in Wyoming and Colorado? Or the express office in Provo? Or the train stop at Elephant Crossing?"

Race slid farther down in the chair so that he was all but reclining, his shoulders barely touching the back. "Forget it. You come up with all the ideas and we take all the risks."

"Let's hear what he's got."

Raising the hat, Race met Jim Shirley's gaze across the table. The cripple was sitting up straight now, his murky eyes level. Behind him stood the squaw with her hands down at her sides, watching them impassively, fully understanding. Then Race saw his cousin in the doorway and levered himself upright.

"Talk, Carroll," he sighed.

The sun lay nestled in a crook formed by two mountains like an orange coal in a blacksmith's iron tongs. Dying violet light stole across the basin and stained the snow east of the soddy with viscous shadow. The horses in the corral huddled together for warmth, their breath curling milky white around their muzzles before the rising wind caught and shredded it like wet tissue. James Blaine Shirley sat on the hut's sunward side with his back to the damp wall and his knees drawn up under his coattails, the tip of a cheroot glowing violent red in the darkness between his hat and collar. Next to him sat Woman Watching, moving only to take the cheroot from between his lips at intervals and knock the ash off the end before replacing it. To the east an early coyote yipped twice and raised its voice in a tentative howl drawn thin as silver thread by the wind and cold. There was no answer and the call wasn't repeated.

"Get it out," said Shirley.

The squaw hesitated, then reached inside her coat and withdrew a hinged leather case from which she lifted a bronze star trailing a ribbon of red and blue silk. She held it up for his inspection. He was still looking at it through his smoke when Merle Buckner came out of the hut, saw what he was doing, and sat down on the other side of him.

"All right," Shirley told the woman.

"None of my business," said Merle, as the medal and case were tucked away, "but I'm wondering why you never hocked that thing. You had some lean times after the war."

"I tried. No one'd take it. It ain't real gold."

"You know what? I don't think you'd of went through with it if they made you an offer. I think you like carrying it."

Shirley smoked and said nothing.

"What you think of Carroll's big thing?" Merle asked.

"It's big." He let the woman tap some more ash off the cheroot.

"I like it. Race don't. I think maybe he's going yellow on us."

"He ain't going yellow."

"You agree with him?"

"What I think won't buy coal."

"Your vote's as good as mine."

Shirley chuckled, without mirth. "It is that."

Merle watched the sunset. Only a molten sliver remained in the notch, forced down by layer upon layer of purple, each one darker than the one below it until they blended with the India-ink blackness hammocking down from above. "You miss them?" he asked suddenly.

The squaw shot him a murderous look.

"Miss what?" asked Shirley, knowing very well what.

"Your hands."

"Would you miss yours?"

"Yeah, for a while. But you got so you get along pretty good without them. I was just wondering if you still cared one way or the other."

Shirley spat out his cheroot. The glowing tip described a phosphorescent arc and died with a hiss when it hit the snow. The Cherokee woman watched it like a bored dog.

"Call you next time I take a leak."

Merle said, "I never thought about that."

EIGHT

Running Behind

The only sign of life in Elephant Crossing at six-thirty in the morning was a pair of drifters loitering under the water tower, their wind-reddened eyes following the seven armed men as they alighted from the coach two cars behind the panting engine. It was still dark out and pump-handle cold. The snow creaked under their boots.

Liquid lantern light glimmered forlornly through a window in the tar-paper-and-canvas saloon. As he followed St. John across the furrowed street toward the light, Wild Bill Edwards was conscious of dozens of pairs of eyes watching him from behind brown muslin curtains and the triangular shadows between buildings. Though he knew Colorado, this was his first visit to Elephant Crossing, and yet he had been there many times—in Texas and New Mexico and the Nations and on both sides of the Mexican border. Only the names were different, and some didn't even have names, these sullen little towns that sprang up in desolate areas like carnivorous plants to devour the lone transient, the winning cardplayer, the lawman foolish enough to follow his criminal spoor within range of their deadly spines. He had learned to tread softly in such places. All of his instincts rebelled against invading them in this manner, like federal troops piercing enemy territory. If this was what being on the sunny side of the law was all about, he wanted no more part of it.

The interior was an oval of dirty yellow light surrounded by shadow, in which stood a bar made from a spider-tracked plank laid across two barrels stood on end and one hand-hewn table, around which three men sat playing poker, gray men in ragged coats without a trace of humanity in their features. More barrels and kegs were stacked behind the bar against a bare wall. The stove in the corner had been fashioned from a boiler with a crooked pipe thrust through a caulked hole in the tar paper. Edwards smelled burning creosote, which explained the spaces he had seen along the railroad tracks where ties were missing. The visitors' heels rang on the hard clay floor.

A lean bartender wearing a red flannel shirt over a faded checked one over another of no discernible pattern or color was sitting on a barrel near the lower end of the bar, with his big, raw-knuckled hands resting on his knees. His shaggy brown hair spilled in an arc over his forehead and behind his ears to his collar. Black beard matted his face from eyes to jaw. He didn't get up as the strangers entered.

The Mexicans hung back at the door while Edwards and George American Horse strolled to the windows facing each other across the room, leaving St. John and Rawlings to approach the bar alone. Midian Pierce remained in the street. The bartender noted all this with dark, malevolent eyes and said nothing.

" 'Morning." greeted St. John.

"Yeah." The answering voice was flat and a trifle high. A double-barreled shotgun leaned against the wall within reach of the bartender's left hand. "We don't serve injuns or Mexicans."

"Who does?" St. John got out the Wichita circular and spread it on the bar next to the coal-oil lantern. "This face familiar?"

"I don't know. Don't look at faces much." The bartender was looking at St. John's.

"We think the fellow this face belongs to robbed the train here Monday."

"That's too bad. For the goddamn railroad."

"The gang was still here when the train left. We think maybe someone noticed which way they rode out."

"No one notices much around here."

"Somehow that doesn't surprise me. Where's the law in this town?"

"Right there." The bartender indicated the shotgun.

Silent seconds piled up.

"Well, thankee kindly," said St. John and turned away, tucking the notice back inside his pocket.

Confused, Rawlings remained at the bar a moment longer. Then he started to follow the old lawman out. He almost bumped into him at the door. The way was blocked.

St. John, who was not tall, had to tilt his chin a little to meet the gaze of the man standing on the threshold. He tapered upward and downward from a huge middle bound by a cartridge belt with a Schofield revolver in a worn holster and a sheathed bowie knife. His beard spilled halfway down his chest and his long hair met the shaggy nap of his floor-length buffalo coat so that he seemed to be covered with coarse hair from hat to heels.

"You law?" His voice rumbled from deep in his vitals.

"You can call us that."

The reply came from behind him, where Pierce stood in the street with his Navy Colt trained on the big man's kidneys.

St. John moved. His victim expected him to lash out with his fists and raised his own. Instead the old lawman grasped the big man's cartridge belt in both hands and heaved, lifting him while he turned his hip and spun on his left heel. The big man went up and past him, completing a shallow half-moon before he struck the bar and tipped it over. The lantern crashed to the floor. Flames lapped at the fragile black stuff of the wall.

The bartender lunged for the shotgun. Edwards' Colt snaked out of its holster, his thumb rolling back the hammer in the same movement. The bartender sat back down

empty-handed. George produced a Starr double-action revolver and caught the poker players going for their own
weapons. They froze, transfixed by its single eye. Rawlings
kicked the Schofield out of the grasp of the man on the
floor. St. John covered the latter with his Peacemaker while
the Pinkerton retrieved the revolver and confiscated the
shotgun. The Mexicans stood around looking mean.

Almost as an afterthought, Midian Pierce strode in,
scooped up a bucket of slops from the area behind the col-
lapsed bar, and dashed its contents over the blaze. Black
smoke billowed throughout the room.

"Now let's talk," said St. John.

Seated on the stump of a fallen elm long since gone to
sawdust and kindling, Paco and Diego Menéndez were
passing a hand-rolled cigarette back and forth in the firelight, speaking rapidly in their bastard Mexican-and-Indian
dialect and laughing in hoarse wheezes. The shadows
scooped hollows under their high cheekbones and in the
sockets of their eyes. Eleven hours had passed since the
excitement in Elephant Crossing. The posse was camped a
day's ride north.

"I swear they're talking about me most of the time,"
muttered St. John, offering George a cigar and charging a
pipe for himself. They shared a bare patch of ground on
the other side of the fire. Rawlings and Edwards had retired
and Pierce was watching the horses.

George said. "They bother me as much as Testament.
They weren't much help in the saloon."

"That wasn't a true test. We had the locals outgunned
with or without them. These bandit types don't waste much
energy. We'll see how they behave when it counts."

"That may be too late."

"That's just what Heck Thomas said the day I hired
you."

"Times were different then," argued the Indian. "Good
men were hard to find. You had to make do with what you
had. It could just as well have worked out different."

"Good men are scarce any time."

George gathered his legs under him and added a stick to the fire. His backside was cold from its contact with the frozen ground—colder than he remembered from the last time he had camped out in the snow. He settled back down, puffing smoke.

"I've been meaning to ask, Ike. How'd you find me?"

"Pretty damn good."

"You know what I mean. It's been ten years."

"I ran into Black Joe Brooder. He said he saw you with Tom Clay's show in Chicago. I sent the wire there and I reckon someone forwarded it."

The Indian looked at him. Orange firelight erased the cracks and pouches in the posse chief's face, peeling away twenty years. "Black Joe's dead," George said. "Someone backshot him when he was marshaling in Arizona two, three years back."

"Two. I had a drink with him in Phoenix in ought-four. That was when he mentioned you."

"How'd you know I'd still be with Comanche Tom?"

"I didn't, for certain. But what else do injuns do these days, except sell pots in the Nations, or Oklahoma, or whatever they're calling it now? I couldn't picture you squatting by the road looking for tourists."

"Well, you sure surprised me. I heard someone named St. John was stumping for office out Missouri way, but I never fitted it to you on account of I remembered what you always said about politicians. I thought you were dead."

"Others thought so too, looks like." The reply was flat.

"What made you do it?"

The old lawman puffed up a great cloud of gray smoke before answering. "I got the rheumatism in my legs, for one thing. Got so I couldn't sit a horse for more than four hours at a stretch."

"You put in lots more than that today."

"Saddle sores kept my mind off my legs," he said, and he might have chuckled. "Anyway, there wasn't much call any more for freelance law, and the permanent jobs were all took. I tried my hand at business for a spell, built up a fair trade buying and selling real estate off the Northern

Pacific right-of-way in Dakota and Montana. Then my partners run out and left me with fifteen hundred acres that
hadn't been paid for. Near wiped me out, but I took what
capital I had left and sunk it in mining equipment to sell
to prospectors on their way to Alaska from San Francisco.
Then the boom went bust. In between there I hauled freight
over the Divide in Idaho, but the railroads squoze me out.
That left just jail and politics. I been to jail.''

"Who backed you for Congress?''

"Some fellows I did business with in St. Louis when I
was in real property. Told me I was the West's great hope
for the twentieth century. Turned out they just wanted
someone to give the Republicans a fight and set the party
up for a solid candidate in 1908. They had him all picked
out, a lawyer from Michigan. I disappointed them, though.''

"It appears we wasted a lot of years running down the
wrong outlaws,'' commented the Indian.

"What the hell, Wild Bill was right. What would someone like me do in Washington? Be like inviting a wolfer
to a ladies' ice cream social.''

Neither man laughed. George flipped his cigar into the
fire. "I heard you got married.''

"That's not all.'' Brightening, the other rummaged
through his pockets and came up with a tintype not much
larger than a postage stamp, which he handed to his companion. A boy of about five dressed in a suit like a man's
looked seriously out at him from in front of a painted forest.
He had blond hair and his face was round rather than rectangular, but his eyes and the set of his jaw were perfect
copies of St. John's. The image was orange and wrinkled
and beginning to fade in one corner.

"He looks fine, Ike,'' George said, handing it back.
"Where is he now?''

"Rock Springs, I reckon. I haven't seen him or his
mother in two years.''

"I take it the marriage didn't work out.''

"Might of, if we ever had one. Her mother moved in
right after the ceremony. She was dying, Fern said. Woman

can't run out on her mother when she's dying. When I finally lit out, the old crow was seventy-eight and healthy enough to call me a guttersnipe one time too many. She's eating my food, sleeping under a roof I paid for, and she calls me a guttersnipe. I don't even know what a guttersnipe is, but I sure as hell know when it's time to raise dust.''

''You just up and left?''

''Took everything that was mine but five hundred dollars to feed and school the boy and rode out. Didn't amount to much more than a horse and gear. That's when I found out for sure about the rheumatism.'' He knocked out the pipe against his heel. Sparks showered to the ground in a miniature display of pyrotechnics. ''I never heard where you took a wife.''

''Did, though. She died.''

St. John hesitated before laying the pipe aside to cool. ''That's a heap worse than having to leave,'' he said quietly.

''Maybe.'' George watched the fire, spotty now among the failing embers. He made no move to feed it. ''What about these kids, the Buckners and Shirley? Where you figure they're headed?''

''Can't say yet. Don't have a handle on them. Testament thinks that bartender was telling it true when he said they rode north with the twenty thousand, and I trust Testament in matters of criminal thought. They'll steer clear of Denver and Cheyenne; Rawlings says the U.P.'s got shinplasters out on Race all over those towns. There's nothing for them in Nebraska. I'm for keeping on going the way we have been.''

''We're three days behind them,'' George said. ''Picking up their trail depends on how far up it's snowed since the robbery and if we don't miss it by a hundred miles when we come out. Who says this posse duty is so tough?''

St. John blew through his pipe and grinned. ''Why you think I'm paying such good wages?''

Pierce, muffled to the ears in a beaver coat presented to him by the God-fearing citizens of Platte's Bend, Nebraska, shifted hands on the icy surface of his Winchester and stamped circulation back into his feet. Nearby the horses wickered and milled restlessly as far as the pickets would allow. He had recognized the voices of St. John and George twenty feet away and for a time had cocked an ear in that direction, but they were speaking too low to be understood. Discussing him, most likely, that atheist and his heathen lost-child-of-Israel friend. But he was used to the ridicule of infidels. Their attitudes would change come the Day, or if the Day was too long in arriving, some day for certain. For faith and industry held equal positions in his regard.

The gusty wind picked up handfuls of grainy snow that felt like ground glass against his face and unprotected hands. Cursing, he turned his back to it. When he was younger he had accepted such discomforts as part of the price of forsaking Eden, but that was before he had lived long enough to learn that not all men shared its cost. He could not welcome pain that others did not feel.

He blew on his hands. It was at times like this that he missed his gold candlestick.

NINE

Layover in Kansas City

Dusk sifted like gray ash through the window, settling imperceptibly over the hotel room's furnishings and its single occupant, stretched out fully clothed upon the made bed. Behind it, dim light from the meeting hall across the street fanned out gradually across the papered ceiling. Shadows as pale as a tenth carbon created a magic-lantern effect in the fan. Fred Dieterle sipped from his pocket flask and watched the phantom show without seeing it. The alcohol burned his torn and healing throat.

His train was scheduled to leave the station next door in thirty minutes. He had checked in only eight hours earlier, ample time to ask questions and determine that a man answering Midian Pierce's description had left Kansas City day before yesterday aboard an express bound for Denver in the company of Irons St. John and five other men. The former sheriff had no idea what the connection was between his quarry and Judge Parker's famous deputy marshal, nor did he spend time puzzling it out. The fact that they were together meant only that he would have to exercise greater caution.

The doctor back home had strongly disapproved of his traveling so soon after the operation, or of his even leaving professional care before two weeks had passed. Infection of his shredded and sutured vocal cords was a real danger, and the cast on his leg wasn't designed for much walking. As if he would ever again be able to bend the knee or speak like a normal man. He had left his position to his deputy and driven the recovered Winton one last time to Lincoln to see if he could pick up Pierce's trail before it grew cold. The county could sue him for the gasoline and mileage. His wife, twenty-six years old and three months pregnant, hadn't understood either and had threatened not to be there when he returned, if he returned. But he was too full of painkillers and delayed shock and Midian Pierce to care.

It was women who remembered the dapper Bible-thumper; plump, starry-eyed matrons who went on about his polished manners and silvering hair, and from whom, once Dieterle had assured them he bore no ill will, he learned, piecemeal, of Pierce's movements since leaving the lawman in a pool of blood on the schoolhouse floor. Men either found him unrelievedly bland or didn't remember him at all. As he lay there absently stroking his ruined knee, the ex-sheriff thought that he had never known a man so thoroughly wicked who affected people in such mild ways.

Considering the impression Pierce made on ladies, it had been something of a shock when his trail led to a brothel on the Kansas side of the river, until Dieterle found that the establishment specialized in underage girls. The madam directed him to a twelve-year-old with yellow hair and the eyes of a woman of thirty. He gave her money, explaining that information was all he required. Under questioning she said that "Uncle Mid" had been gentle and charming, given to quoting at random from "that funny book," but had revealed nothing of his future plans. When she began a detailed account of their time together, Dieterle had thanked her abruptly and left.

It was almost completely dark out now. The fan of light was a frivolous yellow splash on the ceiling, the shadows trapped inside solid and sharp at the edges and moving like bugs in a jar. Metallic, unrelated tones penetrated the window from a piano in a saloon nearby. The city was pausing for breath between the day's hard labor and the evening's hard fun. The train whistle tore through the moment like a bullet through a man's throat.

Immediately there was a gentle rapping at the door. "Mr. Dieterle?" He recognized the bell captain's voice. "It's twenty past five, Mr. Dieterle. You asked me to rouse you."

"Thanks."

He wasn't sure he'd been heard. His voice was a wheezy whisper, air forced through a windpipe with a two-inch section removed from the middle and the ends stitched together. The effort of speaking abraded all the raw nerve ends inside; to cough was agony born of hell. But he heard the bell captain's footsteps moving away down the hall and got up, leaning on his cane.

A spasm seized his shattered leg. He leaned his forehead against the clammy frosted window, waiting for it to pass. When it did he was drenched with cold sweat under his clothes.

He drank again from the flask, capped it, and put it away in his hip pocket. He picked up his carpetbag at the door and moved out into the hallway, floorboards groaning beneath his feet and the out-of-rhythm afterthought of the cane. The bag was heavy, mainly because of the horse pistol he had packed to back up the Smith & Wesson on his belt under the Prince Albert. That was one lesson he had learned from the man he was going to kill.

TEN

The Philosopher's Stone

The Army reminded John Bitsko of a wealthy dowager he had once met at a party in St. Louis. Encrusted with diamonds from her bull's neck to the curve of her enormous bosom, she had begun every conversation, even with strangers, by asking the other person to guess how much she was wearing in dollars. If the partygoer thus accosted paused to reflect on this bizarre icebreaker or declined to take part in the game, she would trumpet out the answer in a bellow that carried to every ear in the room and set the chandelier clanking.

Hardly less subtle was the manner in which his government shipped gold ore from its mines out West to the Denver mint. Under a drooling sky, the spur spiking from the public railway onto federal grounds was flanked by diagonal yellow stripes bristling out from the cinder bed across the new macadam like the fletching on an arrow, beyond which, warned signs bordered by more diagonals, nonmilitary personnel would be shot. To add teeth to the threat, a sentry was posted in full uniform every thirty yards along the right-of-way with a Springfield rifle on his shoulder. Unblooded troops mostly, thought Bitsko, studying their smooth, sometimes pimpled faces through binoculars from the window of his room over a children's dance studio, but troops anyway, young and eager with the blue edge of training still glittering in their erect postures and spotless leather gaiters. The whole arrangement was such an obvious dare, it was a miracle the attempt to rob it wasn't made more often. He placed his stopwatch on the window sill and shifted his weight into a more comfortable position on the chair. Waiting.

Bald at forty-four and slightly hard of hearing, Bitsko made his living repairing and restoring furniture, but in another life he had been a burglar. That was before some idiot on the *St. Louis Post-Dispatch* dubbed him "the Kissing Bandit" for no good reason other than to increase circulation, and the ensuing publicity put pressure on the local law to arrest the perpetrator. They got him in his boardinghouse with a jemmy in his possession and five hundred dollars in marked bills stuffed into the toe of a boot in his closet. He had drawn a year in Jefferson City and had hated paper money ever since.

His cellmate had been a talkative old goat starting the second year of a twenty-six-month sentence for receiving stolen horses, who had bored him with wild stories about his outlaw past. But he had young ideas and Bitsko liked him. When the horse thief was released weeks after his own term had expired, the pair broke into a boxcar parked on a siding in the railroad yard in Springfield, Missouri, loaded six crates of women's hats onto a stolen buckboard, and sold everything but the horses to the proprietor of a mercantile store in Arkansas for three hundred dollars. With the money they went to Denver and opened the business that became Bitsko's by default when his partner chased a troublesome customer out of the shop with an upholsterer's knife and was forced to flee to avoid arrest. This morning's wire was the first Bitsko had heard from him in almost a year. The horse thief's name was Llewellyn Carroll Underwood. Bitsko called him Carroll.

There were worse things than staying honest: recycling furniture was profitable, what with the business boom and prices on the rise, the hours were good, and being one's own boss had few drawbacks when one considered the alternative. For a long time, in fact, Bitsko had wondered why he disliked it so. Carroll's telegram, carefully worded but unmistakably referring to something they had discussed many times in the shop when no customers were present, had carried the answer: he missed the criminal life. Without hesitation he had closed the shop, packed a lunch and his binoculars, and gone hunting for a room that looked out on the mint. His wife was twenty years dead and he had remained celibate ever since, so there was no one to make excuses to except himself, and he was long past that. John Bitsko had rediscovered his true calling.

He was eating a hard-boiled egg sandwich, lifting the binoculars between bites to look down the tracks, when he heard the train whistle. *Gooold!* it hooted. *New gooold!* He chewed rapidly, washed down what was in his mouth with steaming coffee from one of those new vacuum bottles, and activated his stopwatch. He focused in on the far end of the siding. A sergeant consulted his pocket watch and said something to a corporal standing nearby, after which the latter and a private grasped the vertical switch lever and leaned into it, cutting off the through run and connecting it with the spur. Moments later the train hurtled past, the locomotive's oily black boiler glistening like a gun barrel, thorny with men and rifles from a flatcar coupled in front to the end of the caboose. Between them rumbled the tender, a coach presumably containing more soldiers, and three steel-reinforced express cars carrying, it was rumored, anywhere from six to ten million in government gold for refining and coining inside. He couldn't hear the brakes squeal from where he sat, but rubbing frost from the window he saw the steam squirting between the wheels, saw the orange sparks spray and vanish before the train slid into the mint's gray depths, its slipstream lifting the soldiers' waterproof capes. It was gone too soon for ten million dollars, and jaded Denver went on about its business as if the freight were so much grain.

Bitsko stopped his watch and read it. Two minutes, fifty-four seconds from the first whistle blast until the train was inside. There would be another shipment next Tuesday, and again the following Thursday. By then he should have an average.

Two o'clock, plenty of time to go back and get some work done before closing. He crumpled his sandwich wrapping, tossed it into the wicker basket, put on his coat, and stashed the watch, binoculars, and empty vacuum bottle in the various pockets. On his way out he whistled, pausing to don his hat and inspect its angle in the clouded mirror mounted next to the door.

A follower of Hellenistic thought, Bitsko reflected that the alchemists were wrong. The true philosopher's stone had always been the lowly six-shooter, transforming base lead into gold.

ELEVEN

Pinto Creek Hospitality

After two minutes inside, George came to the door of the soddy and lifted his Winchester high over his head, the leather sling drooping from it like a sloppy bowstring. St. John put heels to his dun and cantered across the empty plain, followed closely by Pierce and the others. The sun was a bright new penny in a scraped blue sky and the snow was melting, leaving leprous white patches on the dead yellow grass.

"Deserted," reported the Indian, as St. John swung down, holding back a wince when his boots touched ground and his hip joints locked. He pretended to stretch his aching muscles while waiting for them to loosen.

"Not for long," he said, sniffing fresh manure in the empty corral. George's gelding was hitched to the weathered rail fence.

"There were more than five horses in there. Snow's too patchy to say just how many. Hoof prints are all confused."

"Nine or ten anyway, counting replacements. If this is the right place." St. John's stiffness gave ground grudgingly, leaving needles behind. "What's inside?"

"A marble ballroom and a string of St. Louis whores. What do you expect?"

"It's the right place," said Pierce.

Of all of them, the Sunday school teacher looked freshest: chin scraped pink, burnsides trimmed, clean bandana knotted around his neck concealing his large Adam's apple. Most of the water in his canteen went toward washing. His face was Indianlike under the soft black hat, and with his beaver coat rolled away behind his saddle he resembled a child in a man's cutdown clothes. He would go on looking young until the morning he woke up old. St. John had never known a man with feet so small. Pierce was standing on a bare patch studying the hut and grounds.

"That farmer you talked to said this is the only abandoned homestead still standing for fifty miles," George told the old lawman, plainly hating the idea of agreeing with Pierce. "It's secluded and it is at the end of a good horse's range."

The posse chief said nothing. He looped his reins over the fence and went inside.

After the sun's warmth, the hut felt dank and cold. The calcined remains of a recent fire lay heaped on the floor of the stone fireplace, its lye smell permeating the single room. St. John walked around, touching the springy surface of the walls, stirring the ashes with a crooked stick he found leaning next to the chimney, placing his hands on the back of first one wobbly chair, then the other, testing them with his weight. Rawlings and George watched him from the empty doorway.

"What's he doing?" whispered the Pinkerton.

"Getting the feel of the place."

"What for?"

"Sometimes it tells him what the men he's after are up to. I've seen him do it before."

"You mean like mind reading?" Rawlings' lips curled.

"Kind of. Only with him it works. Sometimes. Not always."

"I'm beginning to think I should have stayed in Cheyenne."

George shushed him.

St. John had been standing in the middle of the dirt floor,

thumbs hooked inside his gun belt, making chewing motions with his long jaw. Now he relaxed visibly, his shoulders slack.

"Anything?" asked the Indian.

He shook his head. "Been too long since the last time."

The others entered, except for the Mexicans, who preferred the outdoors. Wild Bill Edwards exclaimed and picked up something from the darkened corner opposite the fireplace. He examined it and handed it to St. John, who studied both sides. A weary smile broke the stormy surface of his face.

"What is it?" asked Rawlings. The old lawman gave him the scrap. He read the inscription. " 'Five hundred dollars.' This is part of a bearer bond!"

Edwards glanced at Pierce. "How'd you know this was it?"

"It's the place I'd pick." He moved one of the chairs over to the door and sat down, drawing out his Bible. Tiny dust motes swam in the sunlight slanting over his shoulder.

Rawlings said, "Why burn them? They're as good as cash."

St. John flicked a finger at the charred piece. "Say you're a clerk in a dry goods store. Wouldn't you look twice at the man who paid for two pair of overalls and a set of red flannels with one of those?"

"Still, it takes guts to put a match to eleven thousand dollars," George observed.

"We knew they had plenty of those," said St. John. "What we didn't know was that they had this much brains. You recall Nate Blackfeather?"

The Crow nodded. "Choctaw breed. We arrested him for introducing whiskey in the Strip. Judge Parker fined him a hundred dollars."

"You recall how long we looked for him?"

"Off and on for two years. He gave us more trouble than Cherokee Bill and Ned Christie put together."

"He didn't confide in anyone, not even his mother, and he could change skins like a snake," St. John reminded him. "We finally got him posing as a preacher outside

McAlester. Parker figured the United States of America spent two thousand dollars collecting that hundred.''

"Two days later he was back out introducing. We never did get him a second time.''

"He was smart," said St. John.

"He was smart," George agreed.

"Lord deliver us from smart outlaws." He turned to Rawlings. "What's the nearest town?''

"Pinto Creek. North, about five miles.''

St. John strode out, his heavy shadow gliding across the page Pierce was reading. "Let's go see what desperadoes' horses look like.''

Pinto Creek dozed in the afternoon sun, two rows of clapboard buildings snoring into each other's face across a muddy street as wide as a pasture. Telephone wires sliced right triangles between the false fronts and the poles towering overhead. Shiny with creosote, the poles flanked the road like pickets, outriders for the twentieth century. Or, thought Wild Bill Edwards, a firing squad for the nineteenth.

The thawing street sucked toothlessly at hoofs and fetlocks. A butcher, his face sunk in rings of fat like a tallow stub, watched the riders from the doorway of his shop. His leather apron was peppered with blood and bits of raw meat clinging in half circles like pink leeches. He was the only human in sight. Sunlight bronzed a dog sleeping with its clotted chin over the frayed edge of the boardwalk nearby.

A Reo occupied a space where three horses could be tethered in front of the town marshal's office. The Mexicans, who had never seen a motorcar close up, leapt down from their saddles, drew fingers through the powder of dried mud on the fly-green finish and across the grainy leather seats, kicked the bicycle wheels and grinned like apes at their reflections in the shiny brass of the headlamps. Edwards attempted to explain to them through pantomime and sound effects how the vehicle worked. Ignoring the buggylike contraption, St. John and George tied up at the hitching rail and mounted the boardwalk to the office door.

It was locked. A hand-lettered card in the window read BACK IN 20 MINUTES—BUT DON'T COUNT ON IT. On the other side of the glass stood a desk and a black iron stove under a fine coat of indoor dust. A door at the back apparently led to the cells.

"Split up," St. John told the others. "Ask around. Find out if anyone's tried to sell a bunch of well-used horses hereabouts in the last couple of days. Bill, you go with Paco and Diego. Rawlings, with me."

Which left George and Midian Pierce partners. They glared at each other and moved off together without a word.

The livery stable was closed for lunch. There were no customers in either the general merchandise or the bank, just bored employees wearing aprons or watches and chains, their collars wilting from the unseasonable weather's surprise attack on their prickly long underwear. St. John's query drew suspicious looks and the suggestion that they check with the marshal. No one seemed to know where the marshal was. Passing the dress shop display window, the old lawman caught a glimpse of his shadowed jowls and clothes streaked with horse lather and remarked to Rawlings that they had best find the marshal before he found them and arrested them for vagrancy. The Pinkerton, ragged of beard and stained with mud to the knees, agreed. They were on their way back to the office for another look when Pierce hailed them from across the street.

George was nowhere in sight. The Sunday school teacher was standing in the barbershop, watching a barber with spit-curls and a waxed moustache using long shiny scissors to trim the hair around the ears of a clerkly-looking man in his thirties, whose black muttonchops made his face look fuller than it was. The bare steel muzzle of a .44 revolver poked out from under the white cloth that covered the seated man from neck to knees. He wore brown pinstriped trousers over brown leather boots. The barber's hand shook as he snipped away.

The shop smelled of leather and shaving soap and lime, man-smells. A cuckoo clock on the wall next to the smoked mirror knocked out the seconds with a hollow wooden sound against the crisp snicking of the scissors.

"Marshal here wants a word with you," Pierce said. He stood with his hands well out from his body, watching the man with a snake's patience.

"Ask him does he do all his talking over a gun, or are we special?" St. John kept his coat buttoned over his Peacemaker. Rawlings buttoned his, even though it was warm inside with the sun streaming through the clean plate-glass window.

"Who are you?" demanded the marshal. He had a bitten voice. Told the answer, he snorted. "You are like hell. Ike St. John's back East by now, raising hell with the Republicans."

"Weather's nicer here. What's wrong, Marshal? My man here make trouble?"

"I didn't give him that chance." The scissors slipped, nicking him in front of the ear. Blood filled the nick and rolled out over the bottom edge. Without taking his eyes from the three strangers, the injured man reached up with his free hand and disarmed the barber.

"Clear out, Tim. I need both ears to hold up my reading glasses."

Gratefully the barber left, ducking through a curtained doorway at the rear. The marshal stood, keeping the trio covered, and snatched off the cloth, a handful of which he pressed to the cut to staunch the bleeding. He was in white shirt sleeves and a brown striped vest with a gold chain from which dangled a Mason's ring. "Your man said he was looking for someone selling horses. I been expecting that horse thief's friend to pay us a visit."

The old lawman nodded. "So he was here."

"Was and is. I got him locked up over at the jail. Stay back there!" He raised the gun as St. John took a step forward. "You'll move when I say."

"What'd you arrest him for?" asked St. John, retreating.

"Suspicion." He tossed the cloth into the barber's steel basin. The red stain looked artificial on the white linen, like rouge. "He come in yesterday leading four played-out mounts and tried to sell them at the livery. Livery man didn't like his looks and called me.''

"Did he have a bill of sale?''

"That's why I arrested him. It was dated in Colorado just last Friday. Why buy horses just to sell them across the border less than a week later for the same money? I'm holding him till I get word on a wire I sent down to Pueblo this morning. That's where he says he bought them, from a rancher named Wilder. Now I guess I'm holding all of you, too.''

Rawlings said, "I'm a Pinkerton operative. I have identification in my coat.''

"We'll come around to that. Right now let's have your hardware right here on the chair.'' He pounded the brown leather upholstery.

There was a pause. The marshal's eyes set like concrete behind his revolver. It was a Smith & Wesson American, as big and heavy as a boat anchor. St. John was conscious of a crowd forming in the street behind him.

"Do what he says.'' He started unfastening buttons. "Quicker it's done the quicker we can talk business.''

"Now I know how you got to be as old as you are, Pop. Slow now, one at a time. You first.''

Pierce was the last to surrender his weapon. When the Navy Colt had joined St. John's Peacemaker and the Pinkerton's pocket Remington on the seat of the barber chair: "You look like a derringer man, preacher. Flop it down there or turn your pockets inside out if you ain't.''

Reluctantly Pierce added the little two-shot to the pile.

"All right, let's see that identification you talked about.''

Rawlings showed it to him. "I've been assigned to the Buckner case,'' he said. "This is Irons St. John and that's Midian Pierce, one of his men. There are others.''

"I'll be damned.'' The marshal looked from the private badges to St. John. "You really are him, ain't you? Wait till the wife hears I braced Ike St. John! She's always throwing it up to me about how her brother shook hands with Teddy Roosevelt when he was police commissioner in New York City.''

"Your wife's brother was police commissioner in New York City?" St. John was skeptical.

The marshal looked puzzled, then his face cleared. He laughed. "He fixes pipes. It was Teddy that was the commissioner."

"The gun," Pierce reminded him.

He glanced down at the revolver as if startled to find it still in his grasp, still pointed at them. "Oh, sure." He let down the hammer and poked the gun back into its holster.

St. John said, "White of you, considering you got four more at your back."

The marshal paled a little and turned. Edwards was standing in front of the open curtain gripping his sharpshooter's pistol, flanked by the Mexicans. The barrels of their heavy Villista Colts, browned to avoid glinting in the sun, looked like hollow logs in the electric light. Beyond them, framed in the sunlit doorway leading out of the back room, George watched the alley, fingers curled around the butt of the Starr above the waistband of his trousers.

"How'd they know what was going on?" asked the peace officer, turning back. His voice came from just behind his tongue.

"Lessons cost extra," St. John informed him. "Pay for the haircut."

TWELVE

Carroll

A twelve-inch plank formed a sorry bridge across the street of muck, its sagging middle submerged beneath a brown lake so that the ends curved up like pieces of two planks. The party started across single file with the marshal in front. The crowd that had gathered outside the barbershop watched them without following. They looked like a parade in mufti. The butcher was still in his doorway. The dog had moved with the sun to another part of the boardwalk.

"You make it a practice to leave your prisoners unguarded?" inquired St. John when they were in front of the office. He watched the peace officer, whose name was Kendall, sorting through the keys on his ring.

"My one and only deputy's home with the ague. And you ain't seen our jail."

The air in the office was sour with the memory of boiled coffee, old cigars, and older sweat. The marshal led the way through the door in back and up a steep flight of narrow, squeaking stairs to four cells facing each other across a cramped aisle. Solid oak clunked under their footsteps. The Menéndezes had remained outside as usual; a series of beeps out front revealed that they had discovered the Reo's horn.

The lone prisoner was an old man with short white whiskers and long hair hanging over his ears from a fringe around his naked scalp. He was sitting on the edge of his iron cot with one boot off and a sock on his hand, sourly contemplating his fingers poking through ragged holes in the toe. The stale dirty smell of the blackened wool hung in the atmosphere. There were only two windows on that floor, very small and very high up.

"Sure wish you'd give me that needle, Marshal," he said without looking up.

"And let you stick a vein? Besides, who's going to see the holes if you keep your boots on? You're long past whoring age."

"If I thought that, I'd of stuck myself long before this. That ain't it, though. I seen this pitcher once of Bob Dalton after he got hisself shot to pieces in Coffeyville. His boots was off and his toes was sticking through a hole in his sock. I don't mind winding up dead, but I sure don't welcome the idee of someone taking a pitcher of me with my bare toes showing."

"Wouldn't be so bad if you washed them once in a while. I brung visitors."

"Seen 'em. Don't know a one of 'em." He turned the sock inside out and pulled it back on his foot. It was just as black on that side.

"He don't know you," the marshal told St. John.

"I heard. What's your name, Dad?"

"It ain't Dad." He stamped on his boot. There was a crust of dried mud on the rundown heel.

"Name on the bill of sale was L. C. Wood." Kendall clanked the keys idly in his coat pocket. It was a brown pinstriped suitcoat that had matched his vest and trousers before it began to fade. He wore a brown fedora with a brown silk band.

"Well, Mr. L. C. Wood," said St. John, "you mind telling me where you got those horses you were selling?"

"Done answered that one once." Glancing up at the marshal: "Anything yet from Pueblo?"

Kendall shook his head. "Appears your Mr. Wilder is a hard man to get hold of. If he exists."

St. John said, "He exists. This bunch wouldn't be dumb enough to use stolen horses on a train robbery. Right, Mr. L. C. Wood?"

The old man made a perverse suggestion and stretched out on the cot, crossing his cracked boots. Five seconds later he was snoring. He hadn't looked at St. John once.

"We'll take him off your hands," the latter told Kendall.

The marshal looked apologetic. "I got to have something, a warrant or something."

St. John nudged Rawlings. "Hand me one of those John Does."

The Pinkerton produced a flat wallet and took out a paper folded lengthwise. St. John accepted it and gave it to the marshal, who unfolded it, reading it at arm's length.

"He'll need a horse," said the old lawman. "A good one, but not too fast. In case he breaks."

Kendall returned the warrant. "Talk to Carl at the livery stable. Tell him I sent you. If you don't, he might try to stick you with one of them beat-down animals the old man brung in."

"Do it," St. John told Edwards and counted out fifty dollars from a roll into the reformed outlaw's outstretched palm. Kendall snorted.

"Carl ain't never let a horse go for fifty bucks yet."

"Carl ain't never done business with me." Edwards grinned and left while the marshal was looking for the key to the cell.

They jostled him up, ratcheted on a new pair of handcuffs with a spring lock provided by the Pinkerton, and escorted him, sleep-drunk and stiff from the chalk in his joints, downstairs to the office. While the square-built man in charge read and signed the receipt, the prisoner raised his shackled hands to his face and rubbed vigorously, the chain jingling, arranging his senses by main will. The Indian was at the door and the other two, the little preacher and the bearded detective, stood on either side of him.

Carroll had found himself in this position several time before. Though none of the young squirts he had been riding with believed it, he had known Frank and Jesse and Bob and Cole and the rest, had thawed the frostbite out of his bare feet next to Jesse's at the campfire, had smelled their horses' manure and they his, had breathed the rotten-egg stench of spent black powder in Gallatin and Corydon and at the fairgrounds in Kansas City, where that little girl had come running out from nowhere as they were leaving and he hadn't time to turn his horse. Now and then he still woke up with her screams buzzing in his skull. His first arrest had occurred soon after, but he had managed to wriggle out of his bonds and flee on foot while the posse was camped and even the man on watch had fallen asleep. He'd had luck in those days.

Then there were the bonds from which he had not escaped. A year in Yankton for possession of a running iron. Six months on a Union Pacific work detail for attempting to drive Texas cattle over the quarantine line. Two years and two months in the Missouri State Penitentiary for receiving stolen horses, which had led to his meeting Gentleman John Bitsko, the Kissing Bandit. (He wondered if John had got his wire.) Forty-four months in captivity had taught him patience, but more important, they had taught him to watch for his opportunity and throw his noose over it as it galloped past.

They were waiting for the tall one to come back with a horse for him. Outside the window two Mexicans with bandoleers under their coats were fooling around with the marshal's motorcar, one in the driver's seat wrenching the steering wheel left and right, the other standing on the running board, gesturing for him to slide over, that it was his turn. The automobile sagged under his weight.

"George, get them away from that thing before they bust it, will you?" asked the man in charge.

The Indian stepped outside, and Carroll started tingling. A warm sensation, it started in his toes, the toes he didn't want anyone taking pictures of, and crept up his legs to his stomach, chest, and head, driving the rheumatism before it like paste from a foil tube. He had always said that a man takes courage from his feet, not his heart, which was another reason why he believed in treating them with respect. He braced himself.

The Mexicans were fighting over the steering wheel when George reached them. One of them bumped the shifting cane and the vehicle started rolling backward, down the gentle decline in front of the office. The man on the running board jumped off. The car picked up speed. George grasped the edge of the frame and tried to brace himself, his boots clawing for traction on the slimy street surface. Kendall cursed and said the car was town property. The leader said, "Son of a bitch," and sent the Pinkerton out to help. He and the marshal watched from the door.

Carroll pivoted on his left foot, swinging his doubled fists sideways and up at the preacher's jaw. He undershot, missing bone but thumping neck muscle hard with the steel cuffs. While his victim was off balance he followed through with his shoulder, spilling him. The lawmen at the door were turning when he struck them with both shoulders and forced an opening between them. He bounded across the boardwalk, past the men grappling with the automobile, toward the startled horses hitched out front.

"Don't shoot, Testament!" St. John roared.

Pierce—hatless, hair in his eyes, scrambling to his feet—didn't hear him. The long Navy Colt was out of its holster and his finger closed on the trigger. Flame leapt from the barrel. The room throbbed. The plate-glass window shivered, fell in silence, its noise swallowed by the deafening aftershock. He fired again.

Carroll didn't hear the second shot. He lay face down in the mud. The back of his coat smoldered.

THIRTEEN

Magdalene's Children, I

Chloe Ziegler was a survivor. When election time came in Cheyenne and the mayor's people padlocked her front door, she cut a new entrance into the side of the building and was in business again that evening. When a curfew was declared with her in mind, banning all male visitors to the homes of single women after 9 P.M., she hired three wagons and delivered. And whenever the ladies of the Women's Alliance for Temperance and Morality reached for their axes and black bonnets, she repaired to the country trailing a list of clients as long as the Jubilee Trail.

She was nearly forty but looked fifty, a wiry woman less than five feet tall with hair the color of house dust springing out in stubborn wisps from a bun behind her head and a chest like a man's. But she dressed like a frontier woman in sturdy white blouses and dark skirts that swept the ground when she walked, and she walked a lot, always hurrying, leaning forward like a farmer chasing his hat, her high-heeled pumps clicking like a telegraph key on plank floors and boardwalks. Her face was thin, with dark thumbprints under the eyes and sharp lines from nose to mouth. None of these things stopped customers from asking for her, however, and the most insistent were those who had been with her before. Women in her profession who inspired respect as well as lust came at a premium.

She was the illegitimate child of a waitress in a Memphis restaurant and a circuit rider from Kentucky. Her stepfather, a ferryman on the Mississippi River, claimed her virginity when she was eleven, after which she left home and learned her trade in the brothels along the river before heading West at thirteen to pan the pockets of gold and silver miners around Leadville, Colorado. From there she had followed rumors of riches to Virginia City, north to Skagway, and finally south to Spindletop, Texas, before tiring of the nomad's life and opening shop in Cheyenne. Along the way she had suffered two abortions and a broken arm when a jealous rancher from near Lake Tahoe caught her with one of his cowhands, and had her belly slit open by a crazy Mexican whore in a Beaumont saloon. She still carried the scar, running in a thin, crooked white line from her navel to the right side of her pelvis. When men asked about it she told them she'd had her appendix removed.

This year she was set up in a house that had been built by a retired New York State Supreme Court justice and cattleman, dead now, below the Colorado border, on the outskirts of Louisville. It was a three-story frame building with a veranda all the way around and a balcony on top like the ones town girls used to stand on to entice cowboys on their way in from the range. But those days of open solicitation were over. Since Chloe's agreement with the authorities in Louisville called for her not to advertise, she had declared the balcony off limits and turned away sign painters who came to her door looking for work. Instead, her trademark, a stuffed rooster posed in the attitude of crowing, was placed in a front window on the ground floor. Past customers who hadn't been in since before her last move had only to ride around until they spotted that straining silhouette with a lamp burning behind it. Chloe's business sometimes faltered, but it never stopped.

On the afternoon Carroll Underwood died, Jim Shirley's Cherokee squaw was sitting on the front porch of the Louisville house in her man's clothes, cracking the shells of sunflower seeds with her teeth, spitting them out, and chewing the woody meat. Pieces of shells covered the ground around her heavy farmer's boots. When cowboys drifting in from nearby spreads asked her what she charged she said nothing. When they persisted she showed them her knife and they went inside. No one entered or left the house without her seeing. Caruso sang in the parlor through Edison's genius, the Neapolitan's golden tenor nasal and crackling like dry paper. The snatches that reached Woman Watching through the thick panes of glass in the windows reminded her of the death chants heard during her youth in Oklahoma. She spat out shells and chewed the woody meat.

In a room yellow with afternoon light on the top floor, Race Buckner lay under a thin quilt listening to Caruso and watching Chloe hook herself into her corset. The stays scraped together the spare stuff of her breasts and forced it into modest hills over the edge of her chemise. She had a moon-shaped birthmark on her upper right arm that leapt and twitched as she drew the cord taut and tied it. Her arms were muscled like a Sioux brave's. Her body was younger than her face and lighter in color.

"I wouldn't say it was bad, exactly," she grunted, stepping into the coarse folds of her skirt. "The problem with outlaws is none of 'em ever take off their boots."

He frowned down at his boots leaning drunkenly against each other beside the bed.

"I didn't mean it literally." She put on her blouse and buttoned the cuffs. "If you ride horses the way you pay attention to women, it's no wonder you got to replace them so often."

"What do you know about how I replace horses?" he asked quickly.

"The Friday after that railroad paymaster got held up in Utah you, Merle, and the cripple were here wrinkling my bedsheets. I ain't been away from a saddle so long I forgot no horse can go two hundred miles in four days without working up a lather."

"Every time a train or a bank gets robbed it don't mean it was us done it."

Glancing in the dresser mirror, she tucked a graying ten-dril behind one ear. "I only see you when you got hundred-dollar bills, and I only see hundred-dollar bills after something's been robbed. I hear three men hit a train in Elephant Crossing last week."

He watched her sorting through the bills in his wallet on the dresser until she found a twenty and separated it from the rest. It vanished down the neck of her blouse.

"You think too much, Chloe. It ain't healthy, for you or me."

She looked at him, her eyes like a lady butcher's reading a scale. "If you're scared I talk to the law when you ain't here—I do. When the law ain't here I talk to you."

"Loyal."

"All I owe you's what you pay for," she flared. "I was loyal to a stagecoach robber in Virginia City. He comes around two days after the robbery flashing fifty-dollar gold pieces, and when the marshal showed up next morning ask-ing about him, I kept my mouth shut. I was sixteen, I thought that was expected. The posse tracked him from my tent to a cave in the Walker Range and shot him sitting on a Wells Fargo strongbox. They set fire to my tent while I was in town shopping. I left with just what was on my back, but I learned my lesson. No one's burned me out of anyplace since."

"It don't seem right," he said dejectedly. "When I was a kid I read all the dime novels about Jesse James and the Daltons and the rest, and I never read where they was ever give up by a woman. They gave their women money for their rent and stuck up the landlords to get it back, and when the posses come around, the women always sent them in the wrong direction."

She came over and placed a hand on his cheek, caressing the fine stubble. Her palm was soft but the fingers were strong, as if piano wire ran through them.

"I like you, Race. If I didn't I'd just send you to one of the girls when you asked for me. You're smart, but you can be awful dumb. I've had fourteen-year-old farm boys that knew more about the world than you."

He jerked his head away. She reached over and patted the cheek. "There's a razor and soap in the bathroom. I'll tell Violet to bring you some hot water." She left, trailing a sharp-sweet scent of sandalwood and woman.

The bathroom was a converted closet under the staircase on the second floor, just large enough for a sink and toilet in matching bone-white porcelain. Baths were still taken at ground level in a cast-iron tub with water heated on the stove and brought by girls scarcely past school age. The house had no automatic water heater. After shaving, Race went downstairs to the parlor, where he found Merle and Jim Shirley seated on the sofa going over their map of Colorado, stained and cracking at the creases.

"We was just starting to worry about you," Merle greeted. He, too, was freshly shaved and smelled of bath salts. Shirley had bathed and had his whiskers scraped off by Woman Watching in a stream outside of Louisville before riding in and was starting to look seedy again.

The phonograph had wound down. Race cranked the handle vigorously and returned the needle to the beginning of the wax cylinder. Caruso sang.

Merle made a place for his cousin on the sofa. "You must like that grand opera."

"It's loud," said Race. "Next time you plan a job in a public place, make sure there's a lot of noise to drown you out. Better yet, don't do no planning except in private." Ignoring the other's gesture, he drew up an overstuffed chair and sat down opposite his partners. Unlike the parlors in most similar establishments, this one was spartan—a few pieces of comfortable furniture and an upright piano with a shawl on top and a vase of flowers. The Edison was ten years old, one of the less expensive models. No lace doilies or antimacassars for Chloe Ziegler. A portrait of the martyred President McKinley hung over the mantel, left over from the late justice's residency.

"We wasn't planning, exactly," Merle muttered. "Just talking."

Race said, "Let's not do any talking till we see Carroll's man in Denver."

"Hell, half the fun of these things is talking about them before. Jim thinks we should hit the ore train going in. I say we hit the coin train coming out. Coins are easier to carry and get rid of."

Race shook his head. "Gold coins are worse than bearer bonds. These days most folks use paper money and silver."

"You can't burn gold coins."

The cousins glared at each other. Caruso sang.

"I know a fellow in Canada will buy all the ore we can bring him," put in Shirley. "Runs his own assay office and smelter."

"What's he pay?" Merle growled. "Half a buck on the dollar?"

"Forty cents."

"That stinks. We take all the risks, bust our asses hauling it clear up there, and he makes all the profit."

Race said, "The guard won't be so heavy on the ore run."

"That's because they know no one's stupid enough to try and rob it. You know how much that stuff weighs? We'd need a wagon and a six-horse team."

"Two wagons," corrected Shirley. "Double reinforced. And two four-horse teams."

"Two!" Merle goggled. "How the hell much gold you figuring on stealing?"

"A ton'd do it. Figured it out last night, in my head. You get pretty good at that when you ain't got hands to cipher on paper. Comes out to roughly half a million, not counting the slag."

The cylinder ran out. The thorn needle crunched rhythmically over naked wax, louder than anything else in the room. Race stirred finally, getting up to start the cylinder yet again. Then he rejoined the group.

They conversed in murmurs, bending so close over the map spread out on the tea table that their heads almost touched. Each time Caruso finished his aria Race or Merle left his place, wound the phonograph, and set the needle back at the beginning. The tenor grew fuzzy, the high notes lost definition. The light outside the window became golden and then gray. They argued, they planned.

"What you reckon them three are talking about?" whispered the thin blonde with whom Jim Shirley had spent part of the afternoon. She stood next to Chloe in the curtained entrance to the parlor. Her left eyelid drooped, a congenital defect. It gave her a lazy look.

"We're better off not knowing." The madam was looking at Race. Her features were carved from old wood, time-battered and dark.

"That one with the stumps scares me. He wouldn't take off that trick gun in bed. All the time we was together I was scared he'd blow my head off."

"It ain't *their* guns you should worry about," Chloe told her. "It's the ones come after them you need to watch."

Outside, darkness came to Woman Watching and grafted her to the shadowed porch.

FOURTEEN

Personal Effects

"Leave him his boots," said St. John.

Working swiftly while he still had light, Emmett Force Rawlings had had the door to the marshal's office taken off its hinges and leaned against the hitching rail to support the body of the man they knew as Wood, which he and George had arranged in the attitude of standing with his hands folded over his stomach. His eyes were half open, still shining with fluid but beginning to soften to a dull, moist glaze. There was mud on his clothes and a dot of blood in one corner of his mouth. They had washed his face with water from a nearby trough and combed the clots from his beard. He looked as if he were waiting for someone.

"Let them be, I said."

The Pinkerton, who had stooped to pull off the dead outlaw's boots, looked up at St. John. People trickled between them, staring at the corpse. "I have to remove them or the measurements won't be accurate. Washington's particular."

"Look close, son. Don't I look particular to you?"

Rawlings straightened. The old lawman was glaring down at him from the boardwalk, feet spread, fists swinging loose from his worn coat sleeves. "He's dead," said the detective. "What's the difference to him who sees the holes in his socks?"

"Just let the boots be."

"The dime novelists don't mention your soft spot for criminals." It came out sneering.

"You forget I was one once."

"I haven't forgotten."

St. John left him adjusting his Kodak and went inside, where Marshal Kendall was pouring himself a third drink from the bottle he kept in his desk.

"Council's going to have my balls for supper," complained the peace officer. "There's developers looking over railroad property south of town. I been telling 'em how there ain't been gunplay in Pinto Creek in ten years. They walked away from the same deal in Cheyenne when Tom Horn got hung there three years back."

"Some things can't be helped," St. John said. "Anyway, we got your automobile back without a scratch."

"You can buy a new automobile. You cay't buy back a man's life." He waved his glass at Pierce, who was watching the swelling crowd through the shattered window. George and Edwards labored sweating to keep things orderly while the Mexicans stood clear, spectators as usual. A man in manure-stained overalls held up a little girl under the arms so she could see over the grownups' heads. "Preacher there could of helped it," said Kendall. "You yelled at him not to shoot."

"If you ever thought you had to stop someone in a hurry, you'd know it isn't easy to listen and draw at the same time." The old lawman was irritated. "You got Wood's personal effects?"

Kendall drained the vessel in his hand and burped. "Locked up in the woodbox out back. Just his riding gear and a Springfield rifle. Want me to bring it in or what?" His voice was beginning to slur.

"I'd be obliged as all hell if you would."

"Goddamn errand boy," muttered the marshal, setting

down the empty glass. He lurched out through the back door.

"Why'd you shoot?" St. John asked Pierce. "You knew Bill and George were outside."

"He pushed me." The Sunday school teacher spoke without turning from the window. The light was starting to fade. An electric glow sprang on in a window across the street.

"Isn't there something in that book of yours about turning the other cheek?"

"That's the New Testament."

Kendall returned, lugging the rifle and a flaking saddle under one arm and saddlebags and a blanket roll under the other. He dumped everything atop the desk. The half-full whiskey bottle wobbled and tipped over. St. John caught it in midair and replaced it in its glistening ring.

"He had a buffalo robe too," grumbled the marshal. "Didn't bring that or the bridle. You want them too?"

"Thanks, I got one of each." The old lawman examined the Springfield. It was one of the old Army .45-70s, with some rust on the outside of the barrel and a stock that had been shattered and wired back together. It hadn't been fired in a while. He laid it down and turned his attention to the saddle. Bits of bark and sawdust clung to the old dry leather. The initials L.C.U. had been burned into the latigo of the saddle with a hot iron. He asked Kendall about the U.

"I seen that. I thought he just didn't know how to make a w."

St. John made no answer and opened one of the saddle bags.

Kendall said, "You won't find nothing interesting in there. I been through it once."

"You keep it all or did you have to split with someone?" St. John rummaged through the debris inside. Tobacco and paper, a stubby pencil with no eraser and most of the yellow gnawed off, a rabbit's foot, two dime novels with curled yellow covers, both about the James gang. The illustrations billowed with gunsmoke.

"You calling me a thief?" Having just understood St. John's remark, the marshal laid a hand on his Smith & Wesson. Leather squeaked behind him. He turned, saw Pierce sighting down his outstretched arm to the end of his Colt, dropped his hand. Slowly the hammer was replaced, Pierce's gun went home to leather.

"No need to get riled," said St. John, lifting the other bag. He hadn't looked up from his work. "What do they pay you, thirty a month and a nickel for every rat and stray dog you shoot inside the town limits?"

"About that." Sullenly.

"That's not much for someone who could take a bullet next time he turns a corner. Judge Parker paid that and two cents a mile, and if we had to kill the man we went out to get, we buried him out of pocket. There were times if I didn't get a good price for the dead man's horse and gear, I didn't eat."

"Not me. My wife raises chickens and sells the eggs. Weekends I work in the mill, when my deputy ain't sick and can cover for me here. Council pays for the oil and gasoline I burn in the Reo."

"Maybe Wood buried it," Pierce suggested.

"Buried what?"

"Around eight thousand dollars, if the robbery reports aren't exaggerated and he got an equal cut." St. John burrowed through the second bag. More dime novels—the Daltons and the Wild Bunch this time—a worn Remington revolver, three cans of sardines, a razor and a cake of brown soap, and a sheaf of yellow papers thrust carelessly inside. This he removed for closer examination.

"Telegraph flimsies," he said. "What you suppose he wanted with these?"

Kendall shrugged. "Lots of folks grab a handful when they send a wire. Saves time next go-round. He was putting 'em away in front of the Western Union office when I arrested him."

"You said you arrested him at the livery!" St. John was red-faced.

"Didn't say no such a goddamn thing." The marshal

rose to the accusation. "I said the livery man called me. He sold the horses and left before I got there. I caught up with him after."

St. John sighed. "Did it ever occur to you to ask the telegraph operator who he sent a wire to or what was in it?"

"It occurred to me. That's all. They can't tell you by law. It's like opening somebody else's mail."

"Well, it can't hurt to ask." The old lawman dropped the blanks on the desk and crossed to the empty doorway. Pierce fell into step behind him. Kendall hesitated, then put on his hat and followed. He tripped on the threshold but caught his balance before falling on his face.

"You'll just be wasting your time," he said.

"It's my time."

The Western Union office shared a building at the end of the street with the post office and the telephone exchange, separated from them by a green-painted partition that fell two feet short of joining the ceiling. At the door to the building St. John swung around and blocked the marshal's entrance.

"Wait here," he said. "A man of your deep integrity shouldn't see this."

Kendall's muttonchops bulged. "It's my town. I'm going in."

"Testament?"

Pierce, who had been standing off to one side surveying the street, turned dreamy eyes on the peace officer. They were the eyes Kendall had seen behind the Navy Colt. The marshal's jaw relaxed. St. John stepped inside.

The operator was a small man in his late fifties or early sixties with pale red hair above his green visor and a face like lead foil crinkled and left to fade in the sun and rain. Most of his colleagues were of his generation; the spread of the telephone had driven youth away from the telegraph, with its stigma of antiquity. He had a hump the size of a melon on his left shoulder that bent him and cocked his head to the right, giving him a sly look as he listened to St. John's request.

"Sorry." He left the dusty counter and scuttled back to his chair at the key. A copy of the New York *Herald* was open to "Buster Brown" on the little table.

St. John dropped a ten-dollar gold piece on top of the counter. The clunk and wobble brought the operator's head up from the page as if a string had been jerked. The coin was buzzing to a rest when his wrinkled hand covered it and scooped it without pausing into the watch pocket of his vest.

"Time I started organizing." Stooping, he removed an untidy stack of handwritten yellow sheets from a shelf under the counter and plumped it on top. "Got to squirt," he said. "Don't look at these here while I'm gone." He went on through a narrow door at the back pasted over with outdated bulletins, walking sideways like a crab.

It was the fourth one down. St. John knew it at once, even though it was just signed "Carroll" and the message, medium length, made no sense to him. It was addressed to someone named John Bitsko in Denver. He memorized the number and street and returned it to its place in the stack just as the operator got back. The latter's expression was blank.

"You still here? Sorry I can't help you."

"Yeah. Well, thanks for your time." On his way out, St. John thought he heard a dry chuckling behind him, but it might have been just paper rustling.

"How you feel about a trip to Denver?" he asked Pierce when he was back on the street. The marshal was standing nearby.

"He told you?" A fat blue vein pulsed on Kendall's temple. "Maybe I got an arrest to make."

St. John raised his eyebrows. "What for, going to the bathroom?"

The marshal's brow puckered.

"I've never been wanted in Denver," Pierce assured St. John.

FIFTEEN

Cheyenne Station

The Cheyenne office of the Pinkerton National Detective Agency occupied the ground floor of a new brick-front building downtown. There were electric lights and telephones and potted plants and female typists in starched white blouses and black skirts and piled hair and the rattle-bang of new black-and-silver Remington typewriters everywhere. The man who greeted Rawlings and St. John outside the door of his office was forty, going gray on one side of his longish chestnut hair, and wore a thin moustache and a prickly suit of a neat European cut. He introduced himself as Geoffrey Halloran. His accent was British and he spoke in italics.

"*Very* pleased to make your acquaintance, Mr. St. John." He pronounced it "Sinjun." His handshake was firm and over with quickly. "I say, Rawlings, you're looking fit. Regular David Crockett, what?"

Rawlings murmured something noncommittal. There were few things in life he resented more than his immediate superior. The Englishman sensed this and, attributing it to the other's Scottish origins, delighted in bouncing hoary Anglicisms off him whenever they met. Rawlings would have hated him if he came from Edinburgh and wore kilts.

The visitors were fresh from a bath and shave at a hotel, St. John in his politician's clothes and the Pinkerton in his checkered suit. His beard was trimmed back to its former closeness.

"Rawlings said he called you from Pinto Creek," reported St. John. "He said you said to look in on you when we got in. We got a train to catch. The others are waiting on us at the station now, getting set to load the horses."

"This won't take long, I assure you." Halloran pushed open his office door and ushered them in ahead of him.

It was a large room, with a thick maroon leaf-print carpet and built-in bookshelves stuffed with leather-bound volumes on law and the Wyoming penal code for each of the sixteen years since the territory had achieved statehood. The works of Dickens filled the only shelf not devoted to legal matters. Indicating two black stuffed leather armchairs for his guests, Halloran hiked around his huge Empire desk and inserted his narrow buttocks into a chair with a high back mounted on a swivel behind it. In back of him a window as tall as a door looked out on the city and the plains beyond. Isolated white clouds lay like stones on a steel-blue sky.

"I love this life," said the chief Pinkerton. He opened a carved redwood humidor on the desk and offered them each a cigar. St. John declined, displaying his pipe. Rawlings didn't smoke. Shrugging, Halloran took one for himself and snipped off the end with a tiny pair of silver scissors on the end of his watch chain. "Used to work at the Yard, you know. Helped bring some of the more sensational developments in the Ripper case to light. London's *ghastly* this time of year. Damned strangling yellow fog. Give me the clean air out here." He finished lighting the cigar and puffed great clouds of urine-smelling smoke into the clean air.

"You didn't ask us here to talk about London." St. John got his pipe drawing.

"You're quite right. You Americans do tend to live up to your reputation for directness. Very well then. Rawlings told me you killed a man yesterday. I suppose it was un-avoidable.''

"If it wasn't, we'd of avoided it.''

"I suppose all the others in your colorful past were equally unavoidable. Sixteen, isn't it? Or am I behind the times?''

"St. John didn't kill the man,'' said Rawlings, his ire rising. "It was Midian Pierce. And you knew how many men he'd killed when you suggested we engage his serv-ices.''

Halloran's brows arched. They were black, a startling contrast to his reddish hair. (Rawlings had always suspected he used a grease pencil to keep them that way.) To St. John: "You appear to have made a conquest. As I recall, Raw-lings was your most outspoken critic when your name first came up.''

"My opinion remains unchanged.'' His subordinate bris-tled. "But I do have a strong sense of justice. St. John tried to prevent the incident from happening, as I explained to you over the telephone.''

"Yes. You said he told his man to hold his fire. Is this the way all your inferiors react to your orders, Mr. St. John?''

"Let's cut through all the crap, Mr. Halloran.'' St. John leaned forward, speaking around the pipestem in his teeth. "Am I being fired?''

"Oh, no, no, no. I didn't mean to imply that.''

"Then I reckon you'll have to tell me what you did mean to imply. It's all that clean air out here; you get used to breathing it and you get so you can't understand gibber-ish.''

"There's no need to be hostile. I'm merely trying to establish whether or not the killing was indeed necessary.''

"It was.'' The old lawman sat back.

"Very well. I'll accept your word this time. But if there are any more such incidents I'll have to insist that I be notified in writing, along with written statements signed and sworn to by witnesses.''

"And if there don't happen to be any witnesses handy, then what?"

"My advice would be that you find some." Halloran's expression went from firm to apologetic. "I want you to know that I have nothing to do with these strictures. The Washington office is—"

"Particular," finished St. John. "I heard."

"More so now than ever. This agency has a reputation for launching its investigations with a microscope and ending them with gunpowder. It's an image we're eager to change. A successful case finishes with an arrest and conviction. Every dead man marks a mistake."

St. John sucked on his pipe and said nothing.

Halloran changed the subject. "So you think Race Buckner is headed for Denver."

"I never said that," returned the other. "I think it's more than likely that he's not. Not dead-downtown, anyway. Not yet."

"But according to Rawlings—"

"Rawlings talks too much. I'm thinking of leaving him here this trip and letting him do his talking among friends."

Rawlings gathered his long legs under him. "Do that and you can say good-bye to that twenty thousand. I said at the start the offer was conditional that I accompany you."

"That's not quite true." Halloran's lips made popping sounds on the end of his cigar, expectorating thick beige spheres out the burning tip. "The condition was that a Pinkerton field operative go along to observe and report to this office. It needn't be you. Would you prefer a replacement, Mr. St. John? I have several capable young men not engaged at present. If you'd like I can arrange interviews."

St. John considered. "No thanks, Mr. Halloran," he said after a moment. "I'll stand pat."

For the first time the chief Pinkerton showed irritation. "Then what was all that about leaving him behind? I confess that after five years on this side of the water you Yanks still manage to baffle me."

"I just wanted to see what you'd do if I made a hole. I'd of bet my gold tooth you'd jump through it, and I'd of won. I don't think we can do business, Mr. Halloran." He put his hands on the arms of his chair.

The other started out of his own seat. "Just a moment! I'm afraid I still don't understand."

"I used to be a businessman, Mr. Halloran. It didn't take, but I was in harness long enough to learn that a man who won't stand behind his employees can't be trusted. How do I know if I deliver the Buckners and Shirley tied up with a big red bow, you won't find some excuse not to pay me the money we agreed on?"

"My integrity has never been questioned!"

"I believe that. I also believe no one ever asked a rattler if it bites."

They watched each other across the clear expanse of desk, the American stiff-jawed but calm, the Englishman red in the face and getting redder. Suddenly Halloran exhaled explosively. Rawlings smelled his ashtray breath five feet away.

"You're going directly to the station from here?" The chief's voice was subdued.

St. John said they were.

"I'll send a messenger around in twenty minutes with a cashier's check in the amount of five thousand dollars. That should buy me some of your time at least."

St. John rose, extending his hand. Halloran hesitated, then got up to accept it. His palm was moist.

"Hold on to your money till I've earned it," said the old lawman. "There isn't much call for cashier's checks where we're going."

The Englishman blinked. Then, tentatively: "You were making a hole again, is that it?"

"That's it. Only this time you went through her the right way. Keep your powder dry, Mr. Halloran. That's an American expression."

"I'm familiar with it. We never did business this way at Scotland Yard, I have to say."

"Maybe you should of. If you had, maybe that Ripper fellow would be in the ground right now with a stretched neck."

"Perhaps. . . . Oh, by the way."

St. John and Rawlings were at the door. They looked back. Halloran's posture behind the great desk was rigid. "I met with officials of the Union Pacific this morning. They've agreed to place a special train with a private Pullman at your disposal. It's at the station now, with the compliments of Mr. E. H. Harriman."

He picked up his cigar and blew smoke rings. "Settle their hash, Mr. St. John. That's a British expression."

In the hall outside the office, St. John paused to knock out his pipe on the edge of a smoking stand next to the door. A typist Rawlings didn't know glanced at them curiously as she hurried past clutching a manila folder, her skirt gliding along the rubber runner as if she had wheels under her petticoats.

"You ever ride posse before, Mr. Rawlings?" asked St. John, when a door had closed behind her at the end of the hall.

"This is my first one."

"Then here's your first lesson. Don't ever make excuses for the man in charge. If he's any good, he won't need them, and if he's not, he doesn't deserve them."

"If you mean what I said about the killing," retorted the detective, "what was I supposed to do, let you take the blame for Pierce's mistake?"

"I don't remember appointing you my keeper. And it wasn't his mistake."

"Whose, then?"

"Mine. I sent the wrong one out to help George with that automobile. I should of sent Testament and left you to guard Wood. You wouldn't of been so quick to shoot. But I didn't count on him taking Testament by surprise like he did."

"I warned you about Pierce at the beginning."

"I don't like him neither, but he's a good man in his place. You just haven't seen it yet. You will when the time comes. I hope it doesn't." He opened his pocketknife and scraped the bowl of the pipe. "Just remember who's giving the orders, and who's responsible for what happens. I know

I'm an old man, but I don't require nursing just yet."

They were moving down the hall now, St. John cleaning the pipe as he walked. Rawlings nodded to the attractive redhead at the front desk, who had accepted his undeveloped pictures for processing and shipment to Washington. She smiled back. They had gone out to dinner once, but he couldn't remember her name.

Outside, the air was cooling and there was a collar of gray cloud to the west, solemnly promising rain or snow before nightfall. The street rumbled and creaked with wagon traffic hauling bricks and timber; Cheyenne was undergoing another of its periodic building booms amid the atmosphere of national prosperity. Khaki-clad soldiers bivouacking in the area loitered singly in doorways and wandered the boardwalks in pairs and groups, their dimpled campaign hats prevented from sliding forward over their freckle faces by thin black straps hugging the curve of their close-cropped heads. To Rawlings they seemed terribly young to be carrying the burden of a nation's security. He wondered if such an observation was the first sign of age.

"Now that we got our own personal train, there's time before we leave if you want to go home and see your wife or something," St. John said. He exchanged his pipe for a fresh cigar and turned into a shop doorway to light it. A gray-haired woman standing behind a counter inside glared at him. He winked at her.

"I don't have a wife."

The match went into the gutter and they resumed walking in the direction of the train station. "I reckon it's none of my business to ask how come."

"You're right," said the detective shoddily. "None of your business is exactly what it is."

Then he was telling the old lawman about the girl in Charleston who had promised to wait and who, when he came back from the war with Spain, had been six months married and gone. His association with the agency had begun soon afterward, and he had yet to find a woman who was willing to share him with the ghost of Allan Pinkerton.

"Odds are you haven't tried." St. John gave the cigar a

quarter turn at intervals to keep it from burning unevenly in the slight breeze.

"Not really. I enjoy detective work. If I spend the rest of my life married to the agency, I won't think it was wasted."

"Time's a funny thing," said his companion. "You never know you're wasting it till it's gone."

They were nearing the station. A sharp odor of steam and steel reached them on a blast of arctic air as they turned a corner. Rawlings turned up his coat collar. "Did you mean what you said in there about me talking too much?" he asked.

"There you go again."

The special train consisted of a locomotive, tender and caboose, a day coach, a boxcar for the horses, and a Pullman salon car equipped like a brothel on wheels, with everything but the girls. That thought set Pierce to prowling the platform while the engineer and conductor stood outside the cab glumly waiting for the through local to pull out before leaving the siding. White steam exhaled by the champing engine moistened Testament's trouser legs as he paused to survey the knot of well-wishers gathered near the other train. His eyes lingered for a moment on a pretty adolescent girl in yellow dress and bonnet, then moved on. She was standing with an adult couple, probably her parents. There were a few other girls of various ages and appearances, all in the company of older people. But except for them, no females below the age of twenty appeared within reasonable distance. He sighed and boarded the coach.

The air inside was close and he could smell the Mexicans the length of the aisle. They sat together as always, the big one snoring with his slouch hat tilted down to his large and obvious nostrils, the thin one with the scars glancing up at Pierce, then quickly dropping his bright black eyes as if he'd been expecting another photographer to take his picture aboard a train. Pierce suspected that the bandit had never ridden the rails before Kansas City and that he thought a birdlike man in black tails carrying lightning on a rod was part of the service. About what you could expect from a country overpopulated with Catholics and heathens.

Rawlings and Edwards were outside on the platform, and there was no sign of the Indian. He was most likely in conference with St. John in the private car. The Sunday school teacher remembered that they had always kept close company and wondered if some savage blood ran in the old lawman's veins. He sat down in the first seat, as far from the Mexicans as the dimensions of the coach allowed, and put his face near the open window to clear his nose of the stench of chili peppers and bean wind and stale sweat.

The whistle sounded. Edwards came in and took a seat behind Testament, followed a moment later by the Pinkerton. The conductor bawled. The engine rocked back with a sigh, then started forward. The car jolted into motion. The platform began to slide. Pierce drew out his Bible.

This time he didn't read it. He was opening it to his black ribbon marker when he spotted ex-Sheriff Fred Dieterle standing outside. Their gazes locked for a moment before the corner of the depot roof moved between them.

SIXTEEN

Twelve to Denver

Oddly, the first emotion that swept over Fred Dieterle
when he saw Midian Pierce's face framed in the moving window was not hatred or triumph or even surprise, but
wonder.

He had lost St. John's trail in Elephant Crossing. Entering the tar-paper-and-canvas saloon while his train took on
water, he had smelled the foul residue of smoke and urine,
read the black-bearded bartender's face, and divined immediately that the group had passed through within forty-
eight hours. But neither the bartender nor his customers
would respond to general questioning, and his lawman's
instincts had warned him against displaying too much interest in the affairs of others among those surroundings. His
stiff leg made him tempting prey for the two-legged wolves
that dwelled in such places.

The impression he got was that the band had not returned
to the train, but had unloaded their horses and struck out
across country heading north. He had considered, then decided against hiring a mount to follow. Though he doubted
his handicap would interfere with riding, the melting snow
would have obliterated most of their signs and he wasn't a
good enough tracker to pursue them without its aid. Instead

he had climbed back aboard his train and gone on to Denver, then bought a ticket on the express north to Cheyenne. Capital cities operated on rumor and innuendo; perhaps a few questions whispered in the right ears would reveal what St. John was up to and thus render his movements more predictable.

After three days he had learned that Judge Parker's old deputy had been engaged by the Pinkertons to bring the Race Buckner gang to justice, that President Roosevelt had hired him to investigate rumors of a revolution brewing below the Mexican border, that he was preparing to go to South America in search of Butch Cassidy, that he had been asked by the State Department to escort the Kaiser on a hunt for big game in the Badlands, that he was assembling a private army to take Missouri by force in revenge for his humiliating election loss on November 6. Dieterle discounted only the stories about the private army and the Kaiser. As for Mexico and South America, they seemed unlikely in view of the route St. John had chosen. The Buckner theory was of no use at all even if it was true. Which left him back where he had started.

He had taken to haunting the station whenever a train came in from the East, picking out likely-looking passengers and striking up casual conversations while their luggage was being unloaded. If the old lawman lived up to his reputation—and the condition of the saloon in Elephant Crossing indicated that he did—excitement followed him, and news of his actions would be picked up and scattered by the four winds like cottonseeds. But nothing came of that. He was just leaving the depot after one of these excursions when he happened to look up as the express that had been parked on the siding pulled past and his eyes met Pierce's.

His heart actually hesitated a beat. A deputy for three years before making his bid for sheriff, Dieterle had learned not to trust in coincidence, to suspect evil intent over capricious fate. But when the latter stepped up and bit him on the nose he could only stand in awe. The caboose had passed him doing twenty by the time he thought to move, and by then his quarry was once again beyond his grasp.

He hurried to the ticket window, behind which a young man in sleeve garters was stacking and putting away time-tables.

"That train that just left. Who's on it and where's it headed?"

He had to repeat the question in his hoarse whisper before the clerk understood him. "That train? That's Ike St. John's special. He's cleared through to Denver. Talk is he's on a diplomatic mission to Japan for Henry Cabot Lodge."

"When's the next train to Denver?"

"Not till tomorrow night. You want a ticket?"

But Dieterle was already gone, his cane propelling him with thumps and creaks toward the livery where his horse was boarded. The clerk shrugged and went back to his busywork.

The sky, so clear that morning, had been metallic since noon, the dark snow clouds spreading like smelted lead from the mountains in the west to where plain met sky at the Kansas border. The first flakes started very high up, tumbling and spinning for what seemed hours before they floated like pale cinders to the naked dead grass still bent over from the last snow. The air was damp cold and smelled of raw iron.

Merle Buckner flicked a drop from his red nose and sawed disconsolately at his horse's reins, drawing an irritated whinny from the animal that filled him with satisfaction. Unlike his cousin, he had grown up in the city and had never sat a horse until he was nineteen. He had been thrown that time, and though he had climbed right back into the saddle, he hadn't trusted the beasts since and had avoided becoming an accomplished rider out of pure spite. To him a horse was just something a man had to put up with to get from one place to another faster than he could on foot, and for this reason he had followed closely the development of the motorcar. He hoped to own one when the present project was finished. Then he would buy the finest horse he could find, tether it to the rear bumper, and force it to run along behind until it dropped, and then drag what life remained out of it. What Merle couldn't master, he longed to destroy.

Race, riding a little ahead of him and to his left, was strangely silent for an inveterate talker. Merle scraped a rowel along his mount's ribs and spurted forward, yanking back on the reins as he drew abreast. The horse squealed.

"Where we meeting Carroll?" Merle asked.

"Sheltered wash northeast of Denver. Says he hid out there in '96 after they got Bill Doolin in Oklahoma." Race sounded bored.

"Christ, I hope it's there. You know him and his stories."

"It's there. He might stretch the blanket some, but he wouldn't leave us twisting."

"He bringing this guy Bitsko?"

"If he goes for the deal."

They didn't say anything for a while. Behind them Jim Shirley and the Cherokee woman rode without speaking. Leather creaked. "You're generally hard to shut up before a job," Merle said then. "You act like you got your rope on something you don't know what to do with."

"I couldn't explain it so you'd understand."

"That's just a nice way of saying you're smarter than me, and I don't like it."

More silence. Then:

"I don't get no picture of us walking out of this thing still wearing our heads. We never done nothing like it before and it don't feel like us, none of it. It makes you think."

"It makes me think you're just jumpy on account of it's so big. You'll get over it."

"I'm thinking this is one we ought to pass on," Race said.

They had been speaking low. Now Merle's voice dropped to a savage whisper. "You heard the vote. You want out or what?"

"Not unless everyone else wants out with me."

"Seems to me I remember summers at your place when we was kids, and you being the only one with guts enough to climb that big elm next to the crick and dive in from the top. You changed some.''

Race laughed dryly. ''I still got the scar on my head from the last time when I hit that rock.'' He stopped laughing. ''You know how long it's been since they shot Jesse James?''

''How the hell should I know?'' said Merle, after a moment. ''Near twenty years, I reckon.''

''Twenty-four.''

''So?''

''Hell, Merle, it was another century and he still got shot. You read a paper lately? Moving pictures, telephones, electric lights, automobiles—flying machines, for chrissake. Can you tell me what we're doing playing Jesse James when they got flying machines?''

''I'm with you now,'' the other said. ''You passed me there for a minute but I'm caught up now.''

''Figured you would be.''

''You reckon we got enough to buy us one of them flying machines before we hit the ore train?''

Race looked at his cousin's eager face. The snow was falling faster now, in poker-chip–size flakes that sizzled when they touched ground. The younger Buckner grunted and kneed his horse forward, leaving Merle behind in a puzzled condition.

St. John sighed and stretched his limbs as far as the fancy enameled tub would let him. The hot water penetrated to his aching joints, forcing the gray cold pain into temporary retreat. The slight swaying of the Pullman barely stirred the steaming surface.

''Sure you won't join me?'' he asked the Indian. ''There's a spare tub in the caboose, porter says.''

''I only bathe when I'm dirty.'' George American Horse, poisoning the air with one of his six-for-a-quarter cheroots, watched him from the depths of a wingback chair, upholstered in burgundy velvet to go with the carpet and curtains. In his rough trail clothes, the Crow looked as out of place amid the gleaming brass and polished wood trim of the ear as a breechclout at a cotillion.

The old lawman naked was nothing new to George, who had scrubbed with him and others in creeks and brackish ponds from Fort Smith to the Texas border. The flesh was softer, not as dark, and he had grown thick in the waist, but his body remained in good condition, especially for a man his age. The eighteen-inch scar running down his right arm from shoulder to wrist, a souvenir of his first meeting with Cold Steel Stu Channing in a Guthrie whorehouse, was fading, and the Indian was glad to see that the bullet hole he had cauterized and patched by firelight in the Winding Stair country had healed into a pale second navel low on St. John's abdomen. No one in that long-ago posse had given a Confederate dollar for his chances of living to see civilization.

"You still carrying that bullet?" George asked then.

St. John lay with the water up to his chin and the back of his head resting on the lip of the tub; his eyes closed. He opened them. "Which one? The one in my foot or the one in my back?" His dreamy tone revealed that he was on the verge of sleep.

"The one in your back. The one that German rustler put through your gut from up on that ledge. I was there when Judd Lowe dug the one out of your foot." It had split St. John's second toe on the right foot. Long since mended, it looked like two toes.

"Some of it's still there, snugged up next to the spine. It shattered when it hit the hip bone and sprayed pieces all over. Doc in Fort Smith got most of them but he didn't want to touch the piece in my back."

"I remember him saying it was the cold weather saved you. Ten degrees warmer and you'd have bled white halfway there."

"And if that bullet had been rimfire instead of center-fire it would of flattened out against my hip bone and you'd of plucked her out with tweezers that same day and I wouldn't be feeling it every time it rains. How things might have gone and how they went don't have much to do with each other."

A black porter in a white uniform coat came in after knocking and emptied a steaming bucket into the tub. St. John blew through pursed lips. His knuckles whitened on the edge of the tub. Grinning, the porter bowed and left with his vacant pail.

"Why Denver?" The Indian snuffed out the cheroot between thumb and forefinger and put it away in his shirt pocket. "That wire Wood sent could be nothing."

"I'm counting on its being something." Slowly St. John relaxed in the scalding water. His face was red.

"You could have split up the posse, sent someone to check out Denver, and kept on trailing the Buckners. This way it's a gamble."

"I don't favor splitting up. Custer was hunting injuns till he busted apart the Seventh Cavalry, and then the injuns was hunting him. It's a gamble any way you play it, but it's less of a one this way than the other. Even you can't read sign under six inches of snow." He waved a hand toward the windows. Flakes swarmed in the slipstream, too dense to penetrate.

"You didn't know it was going to snow when you made the decision."

St. John said nothing.

"Ask me," George said, "they're disbanding. They got their pile and they're smoke."

"They aren't disbanding."

"How do you know?" Suddenly George leaned forward, peering at him intently. "You know, don't you? What you were trying to do back at the soddy, you've done it. You know what they're thinking."

"Not entire. I know they're planning something, but I can't say what. I knew it the minute I read the telegram. I got a handle on them, George. I haven't felt like this in ten years. Thought I'd lost it." His voice was slowing again.

The Indian sat back. "You've got big medicine, Ike St. John. I didn't know better, I'd say you were part Crow."

Again there was no response. St. John was asleep.

SEVENTEEN

Los Bandidos

Paco and Diego Menéndez had no love for gringos, and what they had seen of their companions since joining the posse had done nothing to alter their view.

They had left Mexico half a step ahead of the *rurales* after the murder of a Captain Finero, worked for a time herding cattle for a rancher named Sperling outside San Antonio, and departed in the middle of the night after beating their foreman senseless and lifting his poke. Too late they learned that Sperling was close to the governor, who immediately summoned the Texas Rangers. While hiding out in a Spanish settlement on the Brazos they heard rumors that a man in Kansas City, Missouri, named San Juan was paying big *dinero* to men who could ride and shoot, stole two horses and headed there post haste, keeping to the back trails to avoid *los rangeros*.

The hundred pesos the gringo had offered them for each week they rode with him represented the highest wages they had ever earned honestly and was a great deal more than they had seen during many periods in their life in the shadows. For this reason they would continue with him for as long as the money held out, or until someone else offered them more. They were *bandidos*, soldiers of fortune, lords of the deserts and the plains, and beholden to no cause beyond a full stomach and loaded *pistolas*. The saddle was their throne.

Neither of them was named Menéndez, nor were they related so far as they knew. Lean, moustached Paco had been born tenth to a family of sharecroppers on the Mexican plantation of Elfego Contrale, whose sixteen-year-old son had been slain by Paco, who crushed his head with a rock when Paco caught him watching his sister bathing in the creek behind Paco's home. In retaliation Contrale sent his men to kill every male he found in their house, rape Paco's mother and sister, and torch the building. Sneaking back from hiding to find his father and three of his brothers dead, his mother and sister disgraced, and the survivors homeless, Paco borrowed a rifle from a hunter friend of his father's and waited for Contrale to appear on horseback on the road to the nearby village. Two days and nights he waited, and when on the morning of the third day the plantation owner came into his sights, Paco shot him six times, reloading between discharges and advancing until the last bullet, fired point blank into his prostrate victim's face, exploded his skull like a ripe gourd.

The first of many name changes followed. Paco drifted from province to province, existing on handouts in Juárez and Durango, picking coffee beans in the *tierra templada*, apprenticing the bricklayers and tailors in the border towns where rich gringos came to buy land from other rich gringos and acquire handcrafted items by the wagonload from peons for a third of their resale value in *los Estados Unidos*. The scars on his face were put there when a Spaniard with a harelip sent his friends to spoil Paco's looks after he learned that the former sharecropper was seeing his girl friend. A week later the harelip was found in his girl friend's garden with his throat slashed and his ears and nose cut off.

Paco was seventeen at the time, and a bandit in everything but name. It was in the caves of Chihuahua that he first donned the *bandoleras* symbolic of the profession and where he met Papa Villa and Diego, who like him had

settled on the name Menéndez. Because Diego liked the
new man, he undertook to tutor him in the art of cattle
rustling. They quickly became friends, and at the end of
two years, when the drought ended in Sonora and the ranch-
ers realized that the weather alone was not responsible for
their huge losses and Villa elected to disband for the time
being, the two fled north together.

Diego—older, larger, his thin legs bent not from riding
but from the same childhood disease that had killed his
brother and sister, offered no excuse for his drift into out-
lawry. He had kissed his widowed mother good-bye at the
age of eighteen to seek work across the border in Texas
and returned for a week's stay less than a year later with
three thousand pesos stuffed in a money belt around his
barrel middle. After that he came back every year, sometimes with so much silver on his person he chinked when
he walked, sometimes with little more than the shirt on his
back, and once with enough lead in his side and right ham
to weight a lamp. His mother said nothing, accepted a fraction of the money he offered her when he had money to
offer, plucked bullets out of him and stitched him up, and
lit a candle for him every night in the church three miles
down the road until the day her neighbors found her bent
stiff and cold over a bowl of half-ground cornmeal in her
lap.

Except to his mother and an occasional authority figure,
he had never lied to anyone about what he did for a living.
Nor did he, like Paco, make excuses to himself or to others
about the nobility of the life he led. Not for him the songs
about great bandits who had gone before—he suspected
they were like him, feeding like coyotes upon rich men's
scraps—or the tales of buried Juarista gold or dreams of
beautiful Spanish women with hair like stretched black
satin who longed for a true man, a *caballero*, to steal them
from the fat dons and their girlish sons. The gold was in
Papa Díaz's teeth in Mexico City and the Spaniards'
women had calluses on their backs from the number of
times the dons had pinned them to the mattresses with their
great loose bellies. They turned away when the wind came

from behind men like Diego. A *bandido* was a thief on horseback, nothing more. He stole because he disliked work.

San Juan, the gringo grayhead who led the posse, fed them well and did not call them names, but he was still a *norteamericano* and not to be trusted. The Indian was an Indian; what else was there to say? He was a familiar part of the landscape, like a mountain eroded into a distinctive shape or a deformed cactus, a feature to rely on, comfortable to have around. Some of his blood flowed in their veins. But the Indian was friendly with the chief gringo and so bore watching. The small man in black had the look of a padre, one of those black crows who existed to stamp the *rurales'* looting and killing with the seal of God; he would not see a wise man's back. They reserved their judgment on the quiet ones, the tall man with the beard and the strange accent and the taller one with spectacles, but did not give them the benefit of the doubt for their silence. Weapons that made no noise were the most dangerous.

Because they rode in trains and did not go hungry, Paco and Diego were content to do their part when it was needed. It had not been at the water stop, where the gringos had moved swiftly and with such organization that the Mexicans were but extra cargo, or at Pinto Creek, where the buggy that needed no horse had bewitched them and given the priest man the opportunity to prove their suspicions about him by shooting that other gringo from behind. Like most untutored peasants they stood in awe of total efficiency. It drew their respect and not a little fear, like that of savages witnessing a cavalry drill. There was a nagging uneasiness that someday that deadly precision would be brought to bear against them. So long as they feared San Juan, they would be loyal. The ranch foreman in Texas had not frightened them and had paid the price of a few broken bones and the loss of his *dinero*. Even coyotes ceased scavenging and turned predators when they sensed easy prey.

Life above the border fascinated them, particularly the preponderance of wealth. True, there were poor gringos, but the poorest of them wore shoes and ate daily. Beds and

glass windows were taken for granted. Every farmer had at
least one hundred and sixty acres of his own to till, and
sharecropping was uncommon. Electric lights were everywhere, not just in the big cities. On a Kansas City street
corner, for the price of five American *centavos*, the vaca-
tioning bandits had been allowed to peep through a pair of
binoculars attached to a machine, turn a crank, and watch
two hefty women undressing in a tiny bedroom. When the
crank stopped so would they, trapped in their voluminous
drawers, each with a garment in one hand; when it was
turned backward they would put their clothes back on. The
images were fuzzy and orange-tinted. They weren't real
women, just tintypes on a spool, another rich gringo trick.
When the man who had taken their five *centavos* refused
to give it back, they had robbed him at gunpoint. His pockets had been full of *centavos*.

Denver was as big as Kansas City, and much bigger than
either Mexico City or Durango, or indeed any other major
population center in Mexico. Perched on a rolling plateau
a mile above sea level, it boiled with humanity and machinery against the close solid massiveness of the Rocky
Mountains, their snow-covered peaks blocked in on a gray
sky, like chalk on a dirty board. Most of the streets were
paved, and the occasional *pop-pop-pop-pop* of a lone automobile dulled the humming and clanging of the electric
streetcars and the general steam-age racket of twelve major
railroads in confluence. Smoke from the mills, breweries,
meat-packing plants, and mint fed a spreading black mush-
room suspended hundreds of feet above the stacks. The city
throbbed with raw life.

Alighting from the coach behind the rest of the posse, El
Tigre Winchesters in hand, Paco and Diego ignored the
curious stares of idle train watchers gathered on the platform as they paused to breathe in the thousand smells of
life in the American West. It even stank of prosperity. The
whole country was a fat, lazy merchant pleading for some
sympathetic *bandido* to step up and cut his purse strings.
They imagined Papa Villa's round Basque face splitting
into its cat's grin the day they brought him gringo gold.

EIGHTEEN

Gentleman John

"John Bitsko?" The square man with the graying moustache spoke politely.

The shop owner nodded warily, watching him over the top of the four-drawer dresser to which he was fitting a new set of knobs. The old saw that the loss of one sense leads to a greater acuteness in those that remain was especially true in his case; though his hearing was poor, his vision was abnormally sharp, and he had spotted the stranger as some kind of law through his window from across the street. The hand inside the drawer Bitsko was working on held a gun.

"My name's St. John. I'd like to talk to you about a fellow you know named Wood."

"Who?" He was genuinely puzzled. "Speak up, please. I'm a little hard of."

"Wood. Maybe you know him better as Carroll." St. John described him, speaking loudly. Bitsko recognized Carroll Underwood from the description. He kept a tight rein on his expression.

"What about him?"

"Well, to start with, he's dead."

The gun almost squirted out of his grasp. Conscious of

the other's close scrutiny, he lowered his eyes and worked the muscles in his arm as if twisting a screw. He swallowed surreptitiously to ease his tight throat. "Sorry to hear it, but I didn't know him."

"You got a telegram from him last Thursday."

There were others in the shop. A mild-looking old gent in a dusty black suit was studying Bitsko's patchwork upholstery display on the wall near the door and a tall young man with a red beard was standing just behind St. John. A pair of Mexicans lurked outside the front window, looking nothing at all like the day laborers who haunted lowertown. He relaxed his grip on the smooth wooden butt to let air in between his fingers.

"If he sent one," he said, "I never got it."

St. John grunted. "I'm fifty years old, Mr. Bitsko. I figure I got maybe ten good years left. I don't figure to waste any of it jerking around with murderers."

"Murder!" Crouched behind the dresser, he had to slap his free hand to the floor to avoid sprawling.

"Your friend Carroll was shot trying to escape. We think he was planning something, and we think you were part of those plans. In this state, any felony resulting in a death is considered first-degree murder, and you're an accessory. You could hang, Mr. Bitsko. You want to talk now or wait till you get to the scaffold?"

The words fell heavily on Bitsko's thickened eardrums. He felt as if all his blood were draining into his shoes, leaving him lightheaded and dizzy. The counter was between him and the others. He started to get up, curling his finger around the trigger of the gun. Suddenly there was a rustling noise and he was staring up the shadowed bore of a Colt Peacemaker in St. John's hand. He froze with his weapon still out of sight.

"I should tell you that if anything but a screwdriver comes up out of that drawer you're wallpaper," the old lawman said calmly.

After a beat the shop owner laid the gun in the bottom of the drawer and rose, keeping his hands well out from his body.

St. John let out his breath, elevated the barrel of the revolver, and let down the hammer noiselessly. The bearded man strode around the end of the counter and plucked Bitsko's gun out of the drawer. It was a Wells Fargo Express, a Colt with a short barrel designed for concealing in one's pocket.

"It's getting late," announced St. John, holstering his own firearm. "What say you close up and we talk over at the hotel?"

The back room had a service entrance opening out on a blind alley. Bitsko, ever the careful ex-burglar, kept a stout wooden crate at the base of the four-foot board fence that closed it off, suitable for bounding up and over. A pursuer, thinking he might choose the easier route to the street, might turn in the opposite direction. "I'll just get my coat and hat." He turned toward the back.

"Coat and hat, George."

In response to St. John's call, a flat-faced Indian in white man's clothes came in through the doorway leading to the back room, carrying Bitsko's outer garments in one hand. A very tall white man came in behind him wearing spectacles. They were both armed. The pockets of the coat the Indian was carrying had been turned inside out.

"Thank you," said Bitsko dryly, accepting the items.

"Wouldn't want you catching cold." St. John stepped away from the end of the counter to let him pass.

Midian Pierce led the questioning.

The Sunday school teacher started by telling Bitsko in conversational tones about Lawrence and Centralia, about the capture of Union soldiers and the methods by which Quantrill's men drew information from them regarding payroll shipments and the location of Yankee gold. The ex-burglar listened grudgingly from his seat on a hard chair with no arms, planted in the middle of St. John's hotel room, but as the accounts became graphic he squirmed and turned pale. The stories had to do with knives and glowing campfire coals and thin strands of copper wire.

Most of the posse had never seen Pierce in full evangelistic fury. By the end of the first session he was in his shirtsleeves, collar undone, face scarlet, the words flicking out like whip ends. Though the volume scarcely rose his voice grew thin and sharp. His eyes shone like pinholes in a lampshade.

While Testament rested, St. John spoke. Without stirring from his overstuffed armchair the old lawman held forth in a soothing rumble, interjecting a question here and there that hung unanswered. Bitsko wasn't listening to the words; he allowed their gentle cadence to flow over him and massage away the harsh effect of Pierce's attack. St. John recognized this reaction and felt sorry for him. He knew what was coming.

Rawlings was fascinated. An admirer of Sigmund Freud, the Pinkerton had realized early the uses to which the Viennese physician's theories regarding psychology could be put in detective work, and here was an undeniable example. Yet he was certain that Irons St. John, with his public school education, had never heard of Freud or his findings. In spite of himself, he felt a growing respect for Hanging Judge Parker's loyal outrider.

The room grew gray. A lamp was switched on, the furnace in the hotel's cellar cut in with a shuddering of pipes. The air smelled of boiled steel from the radiator. St. John fell silent and Pierce picked up where he had left off. The Mexicans, indoors for once, appeared to be listening intently. Like George American Horse, Rawlings was nudged by the suspicion that they knew at least some English.

Dusk became evening. Wild Bill Edwards dozed sitting on the sofa without removing his glasses. Seated next to him, George dismantled his Starr revolver, cleaned and oiled the components, wiped off the excess, oiled them again, and put it back together, reloading last. Room service brought sandwiches for all of them. The Pinkerton took delivery at the door and paid the bellhop. Bitsko's hardboiled egg on rye went uneaten, as did Pierce's roast beef, but not for the same reasons. Pierce was busy.

Evening bled into night. Paco stood guard while Diego slept, squatting on his heels against the wall with his chin on his chest. Rawlings sat on the edge of the bed, contemplating his shoes, with his hands clasped between his knees. St. John ate the second half of his sandwich. The bread was soggy from the sliced hothouse tomato and the meat was tough. They all had their coats off now.

Bitsko broke just after the clock at the head of the corridor outside bonged nine. His shirt had soaked through and his eyes had begun to glaze, and when Pierce stopped talking and produced a flat leather case filled with instruments that glittered in the lamplight, he sprang from his chair, tangled a foot on the rung and fell hard on his face. In the next instant everyone was on his feet. They gathered around the captive, helped him up and righted the chair, and sat him down and wiped the blood away from his smashed nose, and all that time he was talking so fast the words ran together so that they had to go back over it later to get the details.

Five and one-half hours had passed since St. John had entered Bitsko's shop. Rawlings looked at Pierce mopping his slender wrists with a soaked handkerchief, hair slightly askew, face shining, like a Baptist minister at the end of a successful tent revival.

St. John was right, thought the Pinkerton. *I wish I hadn't seen it.*

It had stopped snowing hours before. Accumulation the color of brown sugar from factory smoke made little hammocks on the lower corners of the windows, framing the deep liquid blackness of the night beyond. The single lamp burning in the room highlighted the posse members' features, motionless behind lazily curling blue smoke from St. John's cigar and George's cheroot. John Bitsko lay churning and moaning on the bed, a Mexican standing on either side. Someone had suggested handing him over to the local authorities, but they had no real charge to hold him on and they feared publicity.

"The mint," Edwards mused. "That's got to be a new one."

"It's been tried, but not in a spell." The old lawman

tipped an inch of ash into a tray on the arm of his chair. "One bunch figured to blast their way in with nitro. They buried 'em in one box."

"Captain Quantrill would've passed it by," said Pierce. He was unusually garrulous after his victory. Fred Dieterle was out of his thoughts for the first time since Cheyenne.

St. John said, "That's the trouble with these young fellows. No one's told them it's impossible, so they go ahead and pull her off."

"We showed our hand too soon," George complained. "We ought to have kept an eye on Bitsko, followed him wherever he went. This way all we've got is half a plan."

"We could of done it lots of ways. I didn't hear you speak up when it counted." St. John was irritated.

Pierce said, "They'll hit the train. It'd take an army to storm the mint."

"Yeah, but which way?" Edwards demanded. "Going in or coming out?"

"Who cares? It's the army's worry." George sucked smoke.

"Except if the army gets the Buckners," St. John reminded him, "I don't get paid. And if I don't get paid, you don't get paid."

They spoke in low tones to avoid being overheard by the man on the bed. Bitsko was awake, staring up at the darkness hovering between the globe of light and the ceiling. He was badly frightened. By definition a criminal whose illegal activities demanded the cover of night and the absence of his victims, he had never pointed a gun at anyone before that day, nor had his life threatened in earnest. That man Pierce terrified him with his tales of past atrocities and his case of torture tools. His unadorned language rang of appalling truth. The ex-burglar feared him more than hanging. Much more, because he was sure St. John had been bluffing about his, Bitsko's, culpability in Carroll's death. He lay silent between the darkly watchful Mexicans, his injured nose throbbing, afraid to listen to the conversation, afraid not to, but most afraid of attracting attention and reminding the others of his presence.

"If we tell the army, they'll double the guard and scare them off," George was saying, his voice rising into the prisoner's narrow hearing range. "And they won't let us ride that train without knowing why we want to."

"Unreasonable," commented Edwards.

The Indian said, "We should have held back till they got word to Bitsko. Maybe they still will."

St. John grunted negatively. "Bitsko was expecting Wood—Underwood, whatever—to collect him and bring him to wherever they're hiding. Hell, they could be in Kansas or anywhere else betwixt here and where the gold is loaded."

"Or where the coins get delivered," Edwards said. "They're easier to tote and get shed of."

"Which is why the guard's heavier on that route," George pointed out. "That's the one they expect to get hit. This bunch is too smart to do what's expected."

Edwards' laugh was short. "Maybe they're so smart they know someone's thinking they're too smart to do what's expected and go ahead and do it."

St. John said, "It's like I put a marble in one fist and ask you to guess which one it's in. Next time I might switch fists, or thinking that you expect me to do that, I might leave it where it is. Or thinking that you think I might do that I might switch anyway. You can drive yourself crazy figuring all the angles."

"My God, that's Machiavellian." Rawlings was awed.

"'Tain't neither," rejoined the old lawman mockingly. "It's American sure as you're standing there."

"No, no. Niccolo Machiavelli was—"

"I know who he was. Politicians read too."

"Bitsko knows where they're hiding. I can get it from him if you want."

Bitsko caught his breath. Under Pierce's quiet voice, itself barely audible to the captive's afflicted ears, was a tinkling of steel instruments.

Rawlings said, "What do you mean, 'if you want'?"

"What's left after Testament gets through asking questions generally isn't worth arresting," explained St. John.

The knocking in the pipes grew loud.

"These aren't the Middle Ages." The Pinkerton's voice cut across the stillness. "The agency I represent won't stand for death by torture. Nor will I."

" ' . . . but they shall be as thorns in your sides, and their gods shall be a snare unto you.' "

Something metallic crackled. "Don't throw the Bible at me, you psalm-singing hypocrite."

More silence. Bitsko was afraid to look.

"I was you, I'd pull that trigger here and now." Pierce's statement was a quiet rattle.

"Watch him," St. John warned Edwards. "He packs a derringer in that pocket."

George said, "Make your move or make friends. Wild Bill's arm is getting tired."

Cautiously, Bitsko turned his head to peer through the gloom. All eyes were on Edwards. The electric lamp blanked out his eyes behind the glasses and glowed off the barrel of the Colt in his right hand. No one had seen or heard him draw.

"I think I know where they are," Bitsko said.

There was a delayed reaction. One by one in ragged order, like train cars starting forward, faces turned toward the man on the bed. The former burglar supported himself on one elbow. He was looking at St. John. His heart was pounding hard enough to shake the mattress.

"I'm not sure," he added hastily. "It's just something Carroll said once in Jefferson City. I can take you there tomorrow."

St. John remembered the cigar between his teeth and removed it, spitting out bits of tobacco and soggy wrapping. "Put up those goddamn guns."

NINETEEN

Rawlings' Way

Under a morning cloud cover so thick a casual glance outside made more than one early riser look again at the clock, the lights of Denver glittered randomly like broken glass scattered below the Rockies. The unnatural illumination, smoke-laden air, and strange loud manmade noises unnerved Fred Dieterle's horse, which snorted and shied when its hoofs struck unfamiliar macadam and tried to buck. But the ex-sheriff gave the reins a sideways jerk that brought blood into the animal's mouth and it settled down resentfully, its eyes showing white. Across the city a factory clock chimed the quarter hour. It was past seven and still as black out as widow's weeds.

His knee throbbed under the plaster cast. He had adjusted the stirrup to accommodate the stiff leg, but even so a bolt of blue-white pain shot to the top of his skull every time a steel shoe touched earth. Worse, he was bleeding into his throat; the roadside from Cheyenne to Denver was speckled with bloody spume. That meant a visit to a doctor's office, new stitches, fresh dressing, and delay.

First, however, he stopped at the railroad yard, a rackety place where couplings slammed and whistles shrieked and locomotives as long as the first complete trip by rail revolved on howling bearings all night and all day. He dared not dismount for fear of not being able to climb back up and so conducted his interviews among the captains, off-duty engineers, and roughnecks from horseback, like a plantation owner tracing runaway slaves. No one remembered the arrival of the men he described. "Try the day shift; they come on at nine. But you better see a doc first, mister. You don't look or sound so good."

He slept on a padded table, floating in and out of consciousness while a disheveled and groggy physician mopped his neck with peroxide and sewed over the places where the sutures had worked loose. When that was done and a new bandage was in place, he paid the doctor and checked into a hotel near the rail yard for two hours of uninterrupted rest. He had ridden one hundred miles in nineteen hours, and a few minutes of stupor in an hour and a half of writhing on frozen ground had not been his conception of relief. Never a fat man, he had lost thirty pounds over the past few weeks and was dangerously close to total exhaustion. His clothes hung on him like Indian blankets. He had to use both hands to steady the key before he could unlock the door to his room.

Tugging off his boots in the sullen winter light on the edge of the mattress, numb fingers slipping on the heels, Fred Dieterle was conscious of dwindling time.

The wash, situated twelve miles northeast of the Denver city limits, was as old as the continent itself and had a secret history known only to the men who camped there.

It was gouged into the side of a hill in such a way that it was visible from only one angle, dead south, from where the hill looked like a half-submerged apple with a bite out of it. Glaciers and erosion had carved out a smooth upended bowl with a natural windbreak on either side and an outcropping of thick shale overhead that served as a roof. Northern Cheyenne had used it long before the coming of the white man, to corral herds of wild horses, but by that time primitive arrowheads and shards of pottery were already buried there from a civilization much older than theirs. In the 1880s cattle rustlers had employed it similarly, bottling up strays while they prepared to change their brands with running irons. Robert Leroy Parker, like Race Buckner a young cowboy turned thief, had been among the rustlers in the later days and had used the wash again for a hideout years afterward when more people knew him as Butch Cassidy. Others of his occupation had also seen its merits. Long before Carroll Underwood stopped there on his way west after the violent end of the Doolin Gang, the spot was as popular among outlaws as Hole-in-the-Wall or Robber's Roost, only better, because it was still unknown to the general public.

The walls were of red and black sandstone and grottoed with hundreds of chinks and depressions from which grass grew in yellow tufts and which in summer crawled with rattlesnakes, now in hibernation. There was only one way in, but a sentry posted at the entrance commanded a lordly view of the country without and plenty of time to decide whether an approaching party was worth fighting or fleeing. Scrub trees grew in the alluvial soil on the roof and stretched out jagged branches over the edge that served to break up the smoke of a campfire. When proper precautions were observed, in fact, there was no way an outsider could tell if the wash was inhabited until a bullet knocked him out from under his hat. It was the kind of resting place every bandit dreamed of, designed and built by the god of thieves and brigands.

The Buckner gang wasn't thinking about the convenience of the spot or who had used it before them. While Merle stood guard at the entrance with a rifle, Race sat near the dying coals of the fire splicing rope. Jim Shirley, coatless, shirtsleeves rolled up past his elbows, soaked his stumps in brine water heated in an enameled pan. Woman Watching, who after preparing the solution had cleaned and oiled Shirley's Colt, crouched next to him working oil into the straps he used to fasten the gun to his stump.

Race watched him out of the corner of one eye while pretending concentration on his chore with the knife. He hardly ever used ropes anymore, but he found the work relaxing and often joked that he had braided enough hemp to go twice around the world. Friends of his were always getting new ropes for Christmas and birthdays, and most of them didn't have any use for them either.

Finally curiosity defeated judgment. "What's that do for 'em anyway?" he asked Shirley, nodding toward the steaming pan in which the other's forearms were resting.

"Toughens 'em up." The cripple's voice was tight. The water was very hot.

"Well, it's been eight years. They must be hard enough to bust rocks with by now."

"Pretty near."

"Straps make sores." The squaw kneaded the leather with strong glistening fingers. "Salt heal."

"Salt also hurt like hell," said Shirley, grinning quickly. He smiled as rarely as Woman Watching spoke, and almost never when he wasn't wearing his gun. That was the only time he seemed to think of himself as crippled. Race interpreted his unaccustomed good humor on this occasion as a good omen.

"Hey, we got company."

The acoustics in the wash were such that a murmured word could be heard at a distance of sixty feet as clearly as if the speaker were standing next to one's ear. Merle's statement, delivered with urgency from his station at the opening, brought his cousin to his feet like a purged horse. Cursing, Shirley jerked his truncated limbs from the water and without drying off motioned the squaw to strap on his weapon. "Come on, come on," he breathed, though she was working with lightning efficiency.

Race joined Merle, carrying his Mauser rifle.

"A notch west of that butte yonder," said the older Buckner, pointing south with his Henry. "Sun come out just for a second. I seen a flash."

"Sure it wasn't just a reflection off snow?"

"Snow don't move once it's on the ground."

Shirley appeared, shaking down his shirt cuff over the stationary Colt. "I don't see anything."

"That's the part I don't like most," Merle said.

• • •

"Damn!"

Standing in the mile-long shadow of the narrow butte Merle had pointed out, St. John lowered his binoculars quickly. The sun appeared briefly in a ragged crescent of sky, then vanished behind more gray cloud.

"What's the matter?" asked Rawlings, tugging a brown jersey glove on over his left hand. His right remained bare or it wouldn't fit inside the lever of his Winchester when needed.

"Goddamn sun. I think it caught the glass."

"Maybe no one saw."

"They saw."

Rawlings turned at the sound of Pierce's voice. The Sunday school teacher had a thick woolen muffler wrapped around his throat under his coat collar that made his head look even smaller than it was. He was watching the entrance to the wash, from this distance a pale brown smear on the snow-topped hill.

"If there's anyone down there, they saw," Pierce repeated. "That place is no good to them without a sentry."

"What did you see?" the Pinkerton asked St. John.

"A hole in the side of a hill."

They had dismounted upon locating the wash at last. The Mexicans held the horses while Wild Bill Edwards stood guard over Bitsko, who was hugging himself and shivering despite the furs that swaddled him from head to foot. It had been a very long time since the furniture restorer had strayed far from walls and a fire. With him as guide the group had used up the better part of a day looking for the wondrous natural feature Carroll had described to his former partner and had given up and were on their way back to town when Rawlings had spotted it and cried out.

"They'll rabbit now for certain," Edwards said.

St. John was silent. Rawlings recognized the expression on his face from the soddy south of Pinto Creek when he had tried to read the gang's thoughts. The detective spoke up, looking at Bitsko.

"You said neither the Buckners nor Shirley know you on sight?"

"N-not that I kn-know of." The reply was forced through chattering teeth.

"Forget it," St. John said.

"There's no other way, short of charging the wash," countered Rawlings. "If we do that, they'll be in Nebraska by the time we reach the entrance."

"Then we'll follow them to Nebraska. I been worse places."

"Not lately, I bet," George muttered.

The old lawman found himself massaging his sore right hip and stopped. "They're expecting Underwood to be with him. How'd you explain that?"

Rawlings said, "It's a long ride. I'll think of something on the way."

"Suppose Underwood told them Bitsko's bald. You going to shave your head on the way too?"

"I'll keep my hat on."

"If they don't put a hole in it. Maybe they'll knock you out of leather soon as you get inside rifle range."

"I'm willing to take that chance."

"I'm not. I need every man I got."

"The dandy's right, Ike."

St. John spun on George. "What do you know about it, you ignorant heathen?"

"I'm a Methodist and you know it. Anyway, soon as it gets dark they're going to squirt through our fingers like hot mustard. Rawlings' way maybe we buy time till morning."

"I've gone underground before," said the Pinkerton. "Two years ago I infiltrated the Ku Klux Klan in Mississippi, and the year I joined the agency I posed as a prisoner in a jail in Arkansas for a week to get information out of an inmate."

"You get it?" St. John pressed.

Rawlings shifted his weight. "No. He hanged himself in his cell the sixth night."

"You should of lied when I asked you that. All I ever

get from you is truth. How do I know when that bunch starts pumping you you'll be able to make them believe you're Bitsko?''

"Maybe I won't. But it's a maybe. Their getting away tonight if I don't try is a sure thing. What would you rather bet against, a maybe or a sure thing?''

"I'd rather fold." St. John extended the binoculars.

Rawlings stared at them. "What are those for?''

"They're going to want to know what it was they saw flashing in the sun. Did you figure on telling them it was your smile?''

The detective accepted the field glasses.

TWENTY

Cold Camps

"That's as far as you come, mister."

The shout was scarcely audible, thinned by distance and swallowed in the vast emptiness of the plains. It had been preceded by a pale eruption at the entrance to the wash and a dull *chug* in the earth just ahead of Rawlings' horse, the crackling explosions following almost as an afterthought. He had reined in immediately. The horse tossed its head and wickered, nervous but unaware that it had been fired upon. Rawlings stroked its neck and shouted back that his name was John Bitsko.

There was a pause. The Pinkerton squinted, but the edge of the gully threw a shadow that engulfed his challenger. The sun was two hands from the horizon and turning red.

"Where's Carroll?"

The Pinkerton was prepared. "In the hospital in Denver with a broken leg. His horse threw him."

"No horse ever throwed Carroll," replied the voice. "None ever could."

"I guess no one told the horse."

"What's your bona fide?"

"I'm here, aren't I?"

"Who's with you?"

"No one ever has been."

Again silence. Lowering his lids until the lashes formed a spidery screen across his vision, Rawlings thought he detected a slight movement in the shadow, but it could have been just the sunset breeze stirring bare brush. The voice spoke.

"Climb down and move up. Slow, or you're bird meat."

He dismounted and came forward, leading the horse, his free hand held well away from his body. There was a cold dead feeling in his chest that he remembered from Mississippi and especially from the Arkansas jail; it wasn't so much fear for his own safety as an irrational dread that he wouldn't be able to cross back over to his own side when the time came. Association with criminals awakened something in him that he never felt while actually upholding the law, and it frightened him.

"Stop there!"

He halted two hundred yards short of the entrance, wondering if a bullet was to follow. Moisture trickled down his back under his shirt and coat.

"Ditch the iron."

He unbuttoned his coat with his left hand and slowly drew out his revolver, holding the butt between thumb and forefinger. It plopped into the snow six feet to his right. Next he freed the Winchester from his saddle scabbard and sent it after the belt gun.

"Merle?"

A beat, and then a figure separated itself from the darkness, moving toward him with an awkward gait, as if the legs were stiff from riding. A new-looking Stetson with a brim bent down in front cast a shadow to the man's chin, but his build and obvious inexperience with the strenuous life pointed to Merle Buckner. He held a Henry clasped to one hip in both hands, its bore staring at Rawlings. At ten feet he pulled up.

"Well, turn around."

The Pinkerton obeyed, his stomach crawling. When Merle spoke again he jumped as if struck.

"Hands up."

He raised his palms shoulder high. A hand came forward and patted his chest and underarm first on one side, then the other, and proceeded down each of his legs inside and out, even inside the tops of his boots. The binoculars were confiscated, inspected, and returned. He'd left his badge and credentials with St. John. Clothing rustled as the man stood and stepped back.

"Let's go."

It was warmer inside the wash, where the wind didn't reach and the sun shone coppery beyond the fan of shadow. It took Rawlings a second to link the man standing in the spreading darkness with the picture on the wanted bulletin from Kansas. He looked older, less cocky, and his stubbled face was thinner. He was holding a Mauser in one hand with the barrel dangling. It looked like the model the Spaniards had carried in Las Guásimas. Very likely it had been used on more than one *yanqui* before entering his possession. He was shorter than expected.

There were two others standing near the remains of a fire, one a stout Indian woman with Eskimo features wearing man's clothing, her right hand wrapped around the butt of a Remington revolver like the ones in Race's and Merle's holsters, its muzzle pointed at the visitor. Her companion was a dark young man with even features marred by expressionless flat eyes. One arm was bent. Automatically Rawlings glanced down and spotted a blue bore where the fellow's hand should be. His other stump was crossed beneath alertly. He was in his shirtsleeves, the cuffs unbuttoned.

They were all so young. Even Merle, the oldest, was several years the detective's junior. Suddenly he felt ancient.

"How'd Carroll get throwed?" asked Race. His tone was conversational, but Rawlings knew he was on the grill.

"His horse stepped in a gopher hole on his way to see me. A farmer found him and took him to the hospital in his buckboard. He'll be out in a week, but he'll be on crutches for the next two or three months."

No one said anything right away. Merle, who had collected Rawlings' weapons from the snow outside, strode around him and deposited them on the ground in front of Race. He was a head taller than his cousin and wore a moustache that needed trimming.

"You must be older than you look," Race said then.

"I've been told that."

"You look like a railroad detective, Mr. Bitsko."

"What does a railroad detective look like, Mr. Buckner?"

No response. Rawlings slipped a yellow telegraph flimsy out of an outside coat pocket and held it out. Race hesitated, then accepted it. "What's this?"

"It's the wire Carroll sent me from Pinto Creek."

Race read, Merle crowding in to look over his shoulder.

"That's it, all right," admitted the older Buckner, stepping back. "We helped him work out the words that night in the shack, remember?"

"Yeah." Folding the paper, Race nodded to the Indian woman and Shirley, who lowered their weapons. The telegram was returned. The leader's eyes flicked toward the guttering sun. Then: "Sorry we can't offer you something hot, Mr. Bitsko, but I reckon you know about not burning fires at night this side of the law. How about some whiskey while we talk about this here train we're going to make lighter?"

"I'd like that," said Rawlings, smiling. Then his gaze collided with Merle's and he stopped.

After clearing the cloud cover, the sun dropped behind the butte like a coin through a slot. The day's warmth scuttled away through countless holes and cracks in the landscape and the cold damp breath of darkness chilled the watching posse through their coats and made the horses stamp and blow silver vapor. The snow creaked when the men shifted their weight.

"They're in there, I guess," George commented, whispering as if his voice might carry to the wash more than a mile away. "He'd be on his way back by now if they weren't."

"Maybe." St. John removed his hat, ran fingers through his thinning gray hair, and put it back on. It was one of the nervous mannerisms George remembered from the past. The farther they strayed from civilization, the more of Judge Parker's old deputy marshal manifested itself. "Cold camp tonight. You stand first watch." He started for camp at the base of the butte.

"How come I'm always first?"

St. John kept walking. "Because you're an injun."

"Oh."

Wild Bill Edwards was seated on his bedroll in the dying light, picking lint off a tobacco plug preparatory to cutting off a slice with a bowie knife balanced on his thigh. Pierce watched Bitsko trying to get to sleep on the hard cold ground. Paco Menéndez had retired and Diego was crouched on a rock sewing up a tear in his worn right boot with sinew and a bone needle. St. John lowered himself to the ground beside Edwards.

"I didn't know you chewed."

"Picked up the habit in Detroit." He sawed off a quarter-size piece, popped it into his mouth, and returned the rest to his breast pocket where it wouldn't freeze. Finally he wiped both sides of the knife blade on his pants and put it away in a soft leather sheath on his belt. Chewing: "I seen two niggers carve each other up with homemade knives over a hunk no bigger'n a harness rivet. One died. They gave the other life and last time I seen him he was still doing everything with his left hand. I guess I got to thinking that anything worth getting killed over was worth trying."

"Was it?"

He shook his head. "Wasn't worth getting killed over, either. I ain't seen anything yet that is."

The wind came up, lifting snow from the flatlands in grainy white clouds. Edwards spat. The brown juice crackled when it struck the ground between his boots.

"Hope he don't get hisself killed," he said.

"Didn't think you cared for Pinkertons," replied St. John.

"Sometimes I forget he is one. He don't wear their brand."

"Not where it shows, anyway."

"You're worried about him too, ain't you?"

"I worry about a heap of things," St. John said. "Comes with the job."

"That ain't it. Not all of it, anyway. I heard you two talking a few times. Seems to me I remember you and Bill Tilghman talking just like that first time you arrested me, only then it was him saying to you everything you said to Rawlings. Like a pa teaching his son."

"You talk too much. Just like him."

Edwards laughed and squirted more juice.

"This here's my son. The only one I got." St. John handed him the tintype.

Edwards squinted at it. The light was almost gone now. "He's right handsome, Cap'n."

"You're looking at the wrong side."

He hesitated, then turned it over. The old lawman snatched it away. "How blind are you, Bill?"

"Night blind." He spoke quietly. "I'm fine when the sun's out, but when it's coming or going I can't see my hands. Or when I'm indoors away from a window or just coming out."

"You did all right in Elephant Crossing and again in Pinto Creek. You were inside both times."

"I was going by the voices mostly. All I could see was shadows."

"How long's it been like that?"

"Since before I left Michigan. Lately it's worse."

"What do the doctors say?"

"Glaucoma, they call it. I never heard the word before I got to Cleveland. I still don't get how it works. All I know is it means I should buy a white stick while I can still pick out the color."

"Why the hell didn't you say something?"

"What if I did?" He looked at St. John, not seeing him, eyes blank behind the spectacles. "You'd of put me on the train back to Seminole. How long you think I'd last with

Comanche Tom when he found out his sharpshooter needs a jeweler's piece to load his guns?''

"Does George know?"

"I never told him, but I think he knows. Whenever my eyes got to hurting on the circuit he'd fix tea bags over them in a bandana to draw out the pain. Chaw tobacco works the same way; that's the real reason I took it up, though that story I told you about the niggers is true enough.''

"George should of told me. Christ, it's bad enough I'm too old and we're all out of practice. This is a business for whole men.''

"I'll be whole enough when the shooting starts.''

"So long as someone points you the right way.''

They listened to the wind. After a moment St. John spoke again.

"Shoot me next time I say something like that.''

"I will if you point me the right way,'' said Edwards, and spat. He struck the toe of his boot by accident and scrubbed it off in the snow.

"Something I been meaning to ask,'' he said then. "How is it a shrewd man like you let hisself get euchred in business and politics?''

"I reckon I just wasn't paying attention.''

"Sorry.'' Edwards thought he'd offended him.

"No, really. Problem with both of them is it takes an hour of talk to do ten minutes of dealing. It's like talking to injuns, and I never had the patience for that either. I always left it to George. Only I didn't have George to leave it to in Missouri and the other places. So I got skinned.''

"Funny how you never see a necktie in prison,'' Edwards said.

"Yeah, funny.''

The wind rose, picking up more snow from the posse's camp, depositing it in the wash where the Buckner gang and their guest were preparing to retire, and departing with a queer elemental chuckle.

TWENTY-ONE

First Light, Blue Smoke

Emmett Force Rawlings awoke cold and sore and not knowing where he was or how he got there. There was frost on his blanket and when he sat up the cold air enveloped his face like an ice mask. The air was still and the ground was hard enough to clang if a man stamped his foot.

Someone was snoring. Long ripping noises, each ending in an explosive *pah* and the sour smell of half-digested alcohol. A very pale blue streak in the east limned a blanketed shape nearby, and slowly the events of the previous evening took shape in the Pinkerton's sluggish mind.

They had tried to get him drunk, filling his tin cup three times from the bottle Race carried in his saddlebags to every one for them while they asked him questions about Carroll Underwood and gold shipments to and from the mint. Seeking to trip him up. He had answered with information Bitsko had given him before he left for the wash and, using the darkness to advantage, had allowed most of the contents of his cup to dribble out onto the ground, taking one drink to every two of theirs. Even then he had consumed more than was his habit, but any man who could survive the drinking bouts on board an army troop ship to

Cuba was as good as immune to liquor the rest of his life. Nevertheless his head ached.

He got up as quietly as possible, not wishing to disturb Merle snoring next to him, and drew the blanket around his shoulders. He used a corner of the rough material to wipe his running nose. Felon's manners, he mused, and remembered the stinking bucket that took the place of a toilet in the jail cell in Arkansas. His breath smoked as he moved toward the entrance, stepping carefully around the scattered sleeping forms.

"Walking in your sleep, Mr. Bitsko?"

He stopped at the sound of the voice ahead of him. Jim Shirley's silhouette was a shade darker than the gouged earth at his back. He was leaning against the gully wall with his gun arm resting in the crook of a young cottonwood.

"My bladder's bursting," Rawlings explained.

"Step over behind them rocks in back, then. More men been picked off taking a leak than doing anything else. Seems you'd know that."

The last statement dripped suspicion. Rawlings fell back on the defensive.

"I was a burglar, not a desperado. There's a difference."

"More than I would of figured."

The Pinkerton left him. The area behind the rocks reeked of ammonia. He wondered idly if the woman used it too. Modesty was an early casualty on the scout. His urine steamed in the clear cold air.

He almost bumped into the squaw on his way back to camp. She was bent over, collecting dead brush from the base of the wall, humming some monotonous savage rhythm as she worked. He hadn't heard her getting up and wondered if she had risen ahead of him. She ignored him and he walked around her. Merle was stirring, sitting twisted on his bedroll and hacking up phlegm that splatted the ground viscously when he spat. A sharp stench of fermented barley and vomit stung Rawlings' nostrils.

"You all right?"

At the detective's query, Merle started and slapped the

holster containing his revolver. "Who the hell are you?"

"John Bitsko, remember? We met last night."

"Oh, yeah." He paused, then put away the gun. It took him two tries. He went back to hawking and spitting.

"Merle ain't his best mornings." Race rolled out from under his blankets and onto his feet in the same movement. Rawlings admired his energy so early on a freezing morning. " 'Course, the difference 'twixt his best and his worst ain't exactly fat."

His cousin made a gutter suggestion and wiped his mouth on his sleeve.

"No fire," Race told the woman, who had returned with an armload of kindling and was constructing a pyramid on the remains of the last fire. "We're pulling out, eat later."

"How come?" Merle sat with one hand braced on the ground.

"We been here two nights now, which is one more night than I favor staying anyplace. Besides, we got wagons to hire and Jim has to get in touch with his friend in Canada. You want to do all that in Denver, with my picture and his description on every wall and pole?"

"Where are we going?"

"Nebraska. None of us is wanted there."

"That's on account of there ain't nothing there worth stealing," muttered the older Buckner.

"I'll be getting back to town, then." Rawlings doffed the blanket and started buttoning his overcoat. His gun had been returned and was resting on his hip.

"Why?" asked Race.

"I have a business to run. My customers will miss me if I don't show up."

"What's the matter, you can't take a day off?"

"That's not how I make money."

"I been wondering about that." Merle spoke so low it was hard to catch.

Rawlings turned to him. They were both standing now. "What's that supposed to mean?"

"He heard that pretty good." Merle was addressing his cousin.

"I noticed," Race said.

Shirley joined them. "Carroll said you was hard of hearing, Mr. Bitsko. It's funny how nobody has to raise their voice for you to understand them."

Breath curled in the frigid silence. Though it was still quite dark, the Pinkerton was conscious that he was surrounded. He snatched at his gun. He knew he was too late even as his fingers found the grip.

Midian Pierce was having trouble with the Fifty-ninth Psalm.

Standing directly in front of the butte to avoid being outlined against the paling sky, he closed his eyes and tried to picture the all-important thirteenth stanza, but for once his memory failed him and he couldn't even bring to mind the opening line. In times of stress Testament turned either to his Bible or to his gun, and since the glimpse he had received of Fred Dieterle at the Cheyenne station had been too fleeting to make use of the latter, he had pored through the book many times over the past couple of days in a vain search for words to quell the panic growing within his breast. He had only just now thought of the Fifty-ninth Psalm, when it was too dark to read.

The more he thought about it the greater grew his obsession. Finally, against all St. John's orders, he tucked his rifle under one arm, opened the Bible and struck a match, holding the book in front of the flame to shield it from the wash as he turned the pages. He found it just as the match burned down to his fingers, shook it out, dropped it, struck another.

> Consume them in wrath, consume them, that they may not be; and let them know that God ruleth in Jacob unto the ends of the earth . . .

Then he heard the distant shot.

TWENTY-TWO

Dawn

The night clerk eyed the stranger on the settee over his copy of *Collier's* while pretending interest in Jack London's account of the San Francisco earthquake. He was to be relieved in an hour and wanted only to be out of the hotel and sleeping in his own bed before trouble started. The house detective, an untidy stout man with rumpled gray hair who always smelled of cigars though he had given them up months ago, had just left after stopping in again to check on the stranger; he too feared a disturbance but was unwilling to risk causing one by attempting to eject him. He was a year away from retirement and supporting a wife, a married daughter, and her husband, a law student at the University of Denver.

The east window glowed a diluted rose color, silhouetting the stranger's bony face and stiff leg resting on the low library table in front of him. Indicating that he had been in before, he had asked after a party led by a man named St. John, in particular a man named Pierce. After checking, the clerk had reported that both men were still registered but that they seemed to be out as their keys were hanging on the board behind the desk. The stranger then asked if he could wait. The clerk, suspicious of his lean feverish look and unnerved by his eerie whisper, had been on the point of refusing him when the detective appeared and said that the lobby was open to everyone but vagrants and prostitutes.

He wished fervently that the detective had stayed out of it. A recent arrival from the East, the clerk was familiar with Western lore only where it pertained to violence, and though he had never heard of Irons St. John or Midian Pierce, he detected hostility in the stranger's request. It was all very well for the old man to take a chance, as it would be the clerk who took the blame for whatever happened on his shift.

Fred Dieterle was aware of the clerk's scrutiny but gave it no thought. By now he was used to being stared at, and in any case the people and events outside his own orbit were but shadows. Before Pierce, he had never truly hated, and he was surprised by the calmness of the emotion, by the matter-of-fact manner in which he could contemplate another's destruction. Like a bride planning her wedding he had not thought of what lay beyond the actual event; now that it was a certainty his rage became a dim memory of pain experienced and his mind turned to the prospect of life after Pierce.

Abruptly he stopped dreaming. The picture he saw was of blank black nothing, like the stuff beyond the edge of the universe.

"What the hell—?"

The words came out slurred and tongueless, like a cry for help in a nightmare. As in a nightmare, St. John's joints locked and he was unable to move. Then he was able, the cold gray pain awakening vindictively in his hips and knees and elbows as he scrambled out of his bedroll reaching for his rifle. Dawn was still a pinking aureole below the horizon. George stood against it, hair disheveled from sleep. He was clutching his Starr revolver.

"Shot!" Pierce's pulpit-trained voice was bell clear. "It came from the wash."

"Damn Pinkerton," breathed St. John. "Saddle up!"

The Mexicans were way ahead of him, Diego setting his cinch even as Paco slipped his hair bridle on over his own horse's nose. They were early risers by necessity and their movements were the impulses of instinct. Dawn raids by the *rurales* on the camps of bandits were common in Mexico. Wild Bill Edwards, on the other hand, fumbled his glasses onto his nose and groped for his hat.

"What about me?" Bitsko remained on the ground, his blanket held up to his chin. His voice shook. It was the furniture business for him from now on.

St. John's brain was working now. "Bill, stay here and watch Bitsko. The rest of you come with me." His dun, disgruntled by the early hour and the prospect of work before breakfast, distended its belly as the old lawman buckled the cinch. He kicked it and drew the strap tight.

Edwards found his hat and put it on. He couldn't see the prisoner, much less guard him, and he knew that St. John knew. He wouldn't be able to mount his horse for another half hour unless someone led him to it. Bitsko wasn't going anywhere.

"I'll watch him," he said.

The blankets crackled when they were slung over the animals' squirming backs, the saddles stiff and slippery cold to the touch. The horses stamped and snorted gray clouds. The men mounted, and without having to be told they spread out and circled east to put the sun at their backs and in their opponents' eyes. Snow creaked under the horses' pistoning hoofs.

One of the properties of a .45-caliber revolver is its ability to knock a man down no matter where the slug hits him. Moments after the blast from Jim Shirley's Colt kicked him off his feet, Rawlings lay staring up at the murky sky and wondering if he were dead or just dying. Then he felt his right hand filling with something warm and wet, and then his arm began to throb from fingers to shoulder. Someone bent over him and tugged his gun out of his holster. The Pinkerton hadn't even gotten it free when the Colt roared.

"I think you killed him, Jim." This was Race Buckner

speaking. His tone was more dead than dead calm.

"I sure as hell tried."

Merle said, "He ain't dead. Not from no hole in the wrist." Rawlings' revolver dangled at his side.

Race asked, "Who are you, mister?"

The detective worked his mouth, but the fall had emptied his lungs and no sound emerged. A hammer crunched back. He was looking up the bore of his own gun in Merle's hand. He braced himself for eternity.

"Rider they come."

The Cherokee woman blurted out the warning between gasps for air. She had come running from the entrance to the wash.

Race cursed. "How many? How far off?"

"Six, eight. Sun behind. Mile. Less, maybe. Come fast." Her breath whistled.

"Grab leather." Race was already sprinting toward the horses. "Leave the camp stuff. *Move*, damn it!" He retraced his steps and shoved Merle, nearly pushing him down. The older Buckner had to dance to catch his balance.

Rawlings lay listening to his heart beat, blood trickling slippery and warm between his fingers and puddling around his hand. Merle started to turn away. Then he said something the Pinkerton didn't catch, turned back, and slammed a bullet into the wounded man's chest. Rawlings jerked and lay very still.

St. John spotted the first rider emerging from the gully just as the man fired at him, the revolver shot dropping far short. The old lawman leaned back on his reins with all his might, actually lifting the horse off its forefeet, and while they were still clawing the air he squeaked his Winchester out of the scabbard. The animal was well trained and responded to the steadying pressure of his knees as he took aim and squeezed the trigger. Snow splatted just behind his galloping target. He levered in a fresh round and fired again. This time he didn't see where the bullet landed. One of the mounted Mexicans outran him, moving into his sights.

More horsemen appeared. The two parties were so close

now St. John had to look twice in the gray light before shooting to avoid hitting one of his own men. Testament and the Menéndezes hammered away with their repeaters, the cottony smoke scudding across the scene like ground fog. George American Horse exhibited his usual poise. Dismounting calmly amid swarming lead, he wrapped his reins around one wrist to hold his horse steady and rested the barrel of his rifle across his saddle, pivoting slowly to lead each target before firing. Morning wind caught and flattened the reports. They sounded like dry paper.

And then it was over.

Silence wobbled in and sat down with a thud, smothering the lonely last shots. The riders from the wash were out of range and heading west. They made an untidy cluster on the brightening plain. Spent powder stung St. John's nostrils. Forty seconds had elapsed since the opening report.

A drawn-out grunt broke the stillness and Pierce's horse keeled over, sighing mightily when it struck the ground. The Sunday school teacher had his foot out of the stirrup in time and stepped free in one graceful movement. He leaned down to inspect the animal, then drew his Navy Colt and blew out its brains. The explosion seemed three times as loud as any that had gone before. Its echo rattled behind the horizon.

The posse gathered around Testament. St. John urged his horse forward and joined them. "Who's hit?"

There was a general inspection of limbs and abdomens. George laughed shortly and swung open one side of his coat. Daylight showed through a hole the size of a man's thumb. "I guess there's something to be said for buying them too big," he commented.

The old lawman grunted. "Well, I've planned 'em better."

"There wasn't time to plan, Ike," said Edwards. "You knew they was going to rabbit."

Paco Menéndez had wandered into the wash leading his horse. He called out something in Spanish.

"Rawlings," George said quietly.

St. John cantered into the opening in the hillside and

swung down in front of the Mexican, who was standing over a prostrate figure. He knew instantly that the Pinkerton was dead. A grease of blood covered the front of his shirt and his right arm lay in a coagulating pool. His eyes gleamed dully behind his lashes.

"Damn," said St. John.

Rawlings' mouth twitched. St. John felt a surge of hope, then remembered that a body dies from the inside out, a long, disorderly process, and then the real emptiness opened inside him.

"Damn me later," Rawlings whispered, "when I'm dead." His lips were still moving when he lost consciousness.

TWENTY-THREE

Testament

The bullet was lodged in the web of muscle under Rawlings' sternum on the left side, two inches above the heart. St. John made no attempt to remove it, but with George's help cleaned and dressed the wound from the medical kit in his saddlebags. The injury to the Pinkerton's arm turned out to be nothing more than a deep crease on the inside of the wrist, missing the artery, and was repaired in short order with alcohol and a bandage.

"We've got a chance in ten of getting him to a doctor," George pointed out, as the old lawman was covering Rawlings with his blanket. "Bullet's too close to the heart. One good bump and all we'll need's a shovel."

"That's why he's not going to the doctor. The doctor's coming here. Go back and fetch Wild Bill."

"He's fetched already."

At Edwards' call St. John looked up. The sharpshooter was just entering the wash, leading his horse. It was light out now.

"Where's Bitsko?"

"By now? Halfway back to Denver." Edwards produced a clean handkerchief and mopped the lenses of his spectacles. Without them his eyes were a sharp naked blue. "I

figured you was done with him. How close to dead is he?''
He nodded toward the unconscious man.

''That's up to you.'' St. John rose. ''Go to town and
bring back a doc. Hogtie him if you have to. Tell him to
bring a wagon.''

''What about the Buckners?''

''I'm sending George and the rest after them. I'll stay
here with Rawlings.''

''Don't, Cap'n. Don't make me an errand boy.''

Opposition was not new to the former deputy marshal,
who had shot a man in Guthrie for refusing to obey a direct
order. For an electric moment he hovered between words
and action. Then he let out his breath and turned to Pierce.

''Testament, you're the best persuader. That doc might
not want to come. Change his mind.''

''What'll I do for a horse?'' Pierce appeared disappointed at the prospect of saving a life rather than claiming
one.

''Use mine. I won't be needing it right off. Get one for
yourself in town and bring back mine.''

''What about money?''

St. John flared, ''Sell that goddamn derringer if you're
busted. You think I'd be out here if I had any? Quit burning
daylight and go.''

The preacher fixed him with a long look that made him
feel like the lowest sinner in the tent, then accepted the
reins to St. John's dun from one of the Mexicans and
mounted. Wheeling, he kicked snow and dirt over the old
lawman's pantlegs.

George, who had left for a few minutes, barely avoided
being run down by the galloping Pierce on his way back
in. He showed St. John a smear of blood on his fingers.

''I thought I saw one of them jump out there,'' the Indian
said. ''I was shooting, but I can't say who it was hit him.''

St. John nodded. ''You're in charge, George. Tree 'em.''

''Thought you didn't favor splitting up.''

''If I went around doing things I favored all the time
instead of the ones I didn't, I'd still be in Kansas City.''
He laid his arm across George's shoulders and walked him

away from the others. "Watch your back. These kids are smart, and now they've tasted blood they'll be as bad as Ned Christie. Don't give them any slack, but don't push them so hard they turn and bite when you're not ready."

"I'm not seventeen anymore, Ike. I button my own pants and everything."

"Doesn't hurt to be reminded now and then."

The Crow wasn't sure how to react. St. John had never touched him before; he wasn't that kind. They swung back in the other direction and the old lawman withdrew his arm.

"Thanks, Cap'n." Edwards was looking down at him from his saddle.

St. John stepped up close to him. His voice dropped to a murmur. "You're young enough to go on to better things. Don't make the mistake of liking someone so much you go against the odds."

"Cap'n, you and me been going against the odds since the day the midwife slapped us on the ass."

George swung into leather. The Mexicans were already mounted. He glanced at St. John, down on one knee beside Rawlings, adjusting the blanket. The sun was shooting knife-edge rays above the flats to the east and a bar of yellow light lay across St. John's shoulders. Despite the spreading warmth a cold hand closed itself around the Indian's heart. He couldn't shake the conviction that he was looking at him for the last time.

The sunlight threw a grid over Dieterle's sleeping form, warming him into wakefulness. As he glanced around at the empty lobby his first thought was the last one he had had before dozing off, and indeed his only one since his crippling. His clothes felt greasy against his flesh and when he looked down at the watch in his hand his chin scratched his chest through his open collar. His leg ached, but he was used to that.

There was no one standing behind the desk. Alarmed that Pierce may have walked past him while he was asleep, the ex-sheriff levered himself up off the settee, fumbled his cane under him, and approached the desk. Pierce's key was still in place. He reached over and lifted it off its peg.

On the second floor he unlocked the door to the room and stepped inside. The bed was neat and there was no sign that anyone had been in recently other than the maid. Leaving the door open, he went back down to the lobby, replaced the key, and returned to the room. He locked the door from inside and sat down to wait, resting his gun on his thigh.

Pierce found the doctor more cooperative than expected, especially after producing his Colt and threatening to shoot all the patients in his waiting room. The room was soon empty and the physician started dumping equipment into his bag. Pierce accompanied him to the livery stable, hired a serviceable mount, and left while a wagon and team were being readied to go back to the hotel for ammunition. He had expended much of his at the wash.

The day clerk greeted the guest brightly and handed him his key, reporting that there were no messages. He had come on duty while Dieterle was asleep in the lobby and had been in the bathroom when the ex-sheriff awoke and went upstairs. The night clerk had said nothing about him and the hotel detective was sleeping in his room on the ground floor.

When Pierce reached the second-floor landing he halted. A shaft of morning sunlight lay at his feet, illuminating a circular depression the size of a quarter in the maroon carpet. Canes with rubber tips made such marks.

For a wild moment the old panic seized him. He had felt it only twice before, the night he was captured following Lee's surrender and when he saw Dieterle at the depot in Cheyenne. He wanted to cut and run, and he actually did turn. Then the hysteria drained away. He felt his face grow warm as the blood returned, and with it his confidence. He took a deep breath, released it slowly. The last vestiges of panic fled. Grasping the butt of his gun, he crept forward on the balls of his feet until he reached his door.

●   ●   ●

Dieterle heard the floorboards shifting under Pierce's weight and stood up, his heart crashing. Others had passed the door since he had taken up his vigil; each time he had risen with revolver in hand, only to sink back down into a morass of perspiration as the footsteps continued down the hall. But this time the footsteps paused and he knew they belonged to Midian Pierce. He thrust the gun under one arm, mopped his palm off on his pantleg, and took up the gun again. The butt grew slippery almost immediately. Only dimly did he realize that he was standing without the aid of his cane. The pain in his leg belonged to someone else. His heart hurled itself against his breastbone.

The key rattled in the lock. He opened fire.

Four bullets splintered through the heavy door, exposing yellow wood under the brown varnish and knocking gold-papered plaster off the wall opposite. Pierce, flattened against the wall next to the door, grunted loudly and struck the floor rolling. His body made a convincing thud, but he came up again on the other side of the door and drew the long-barreled revolver.

Black, acrid smoke rolled through the room, obscuring the riddled door and burning Fred Dieterle's eyes. He was rubbing his sleeve across them when he heard the groan and thud. Snatching up his cane, he vaulted forward, clawed at the knob, found the door still locked, cursed under his breath and turned the latch.

Pierce was grinning at him when he tore open the door. His Navy Colt barked twice, both times into the ex-sheriff's belly.

The hotel detective slept through the opening salvo. He stirred in the louder silence that followed, and when the two spaced shots sounded a moment later he rolled onto his stockinged feet, rubbed both hands over his puffy face, and reached for his battered bulldog pistol on the bedside table.

Lurching out into the lobby, he found the clerk standing

at the foot of the stairs looking up. A glance at the young man's pale features told him he was no source of information. The detective shoved him aside roughly, taking the steps two at a time as he hadn't since he was a boy. He was still too groggy to be cautious.

There would be no miraculous recovery for Dieterle this time. Pierce knew that as he watched him writhing on the floor at his feet, dark blood welling between the fingers clasped on his midsection. But he had learned to take nothing for granted. Stepping aside to avoid soiling himself, the Sunday school teacher placed the Colt's muzzle to his victim's forehead and blew out his brains as he had his injured horse's earlier.

He realized suddenly that he wasn't alone. A heavyset old man stood shoeless and in his shirtsleeves at the end of the hall, staring open-mouthed at the twitching body on the carpet. A blunt gray handgun dangled forgotten at his side. Pierce shot him through the chest at twelve paces. The old man hiccoughed and fell to his knees. Pierce walked past him, not bothering to turn to see him collapse the rest of the way.

There were no back stairs. Testament peered around the corner, saw no guns waiting for him, and walked boldly down the staircase gripping the Colt. The clerk raised his hands jerkily and backed away. He was all eyes and mouth and white shirt showing between his vest and belt. Covering him, Pierce backed across the lobby and sidled out the front door—straight into a crowd pressing toward the entrance.

Again the panic rose; again he forced it down by main will. Most of the people couldn't see the gun, and those who could were unable to get away from it because of the pressure from behind. He pointed it skyward and loosed a shot. Shouts went up, a woman screamed. A path opened before him. He dived through.

The morning street traffic was at its height. He narrowly missed being run down by a brewer's dray when he stepped off the walk almost into its path. The driver hurled a curse at him and sawed at his panicky team's traces as it rocked past, spraying Pierce with mud and slush.

Out of the corner of one eye the fugitive spotted a flash of blue uniform between two horses passing on the street. Denver had an organized police force. Pierce lost his head and fired. A horse screamed and reared, struck behind the shoulder. Pierce started running down the street, splashing through puddles ankle deep. His boots squished.

Alerted by the reports, two uniformed policemen came sprinting along the walk toward the corner, guns exposed. One of them saw Pierce and shouted. Pierce pointed his Navy Colt and squeezed the trigger. The hammer snapped on an empty shell. The officers returned fire, one explosion echoing the other, *kish-bang*, like a musket report. A hot fist slammed into Pierce's side. He gasped, faltered, and almost fell, but his momentum saved him; he caught his balance on the run. The walks were as busy as the street. The officers couldn't risk shooting again for fear of hitting an innocent bystander.

Pierce's side was wet. He felt himself weakening. His breath sawed in his throat and his chest ached. He bounded up onto the walk, nearly tripping over the edge, and ran into a slot between buildings scarcely broad enough for a man. For once in his life he thanked God for making him small. He threw away the useless Colt and clawed the two-shot derringer out of his pocket. His blood pattered on the alley's unpaved surface.

The passage opened into a courtyard ringed solidly with brick buildings.

He paused, looking around wildly. Then he dashed across, his boots slipping and sliding on loose gravel, seized the tarnished brass handle of a delivery door, and yanked. It didn't give. His side tore open and more blood dumped down his hip. He fell against the door, whimpering.

Gravel crunched behind him. He wheeled, fired. The .41 slug sped past an old man in a greasy white apron standing in an open doorway off the alley holding a full trash can. The old man froze, gaping at the armed and bloody stranger. Pierce cried out and started for the opening. Releasing the can with a crash, the old man leapt back inside. The door slammed. Testament was halfway across the courtyard when he heard the lock snap. He came to a stop in the middle, head down, the belly gun hanging loose in his hand. He scarcely had strength to hold it.

Rapid footsteps entered the alley. He lifted his head and saw blue at the other end.

" 'And it came to pass, when all the kings which were on this side Jordan, in the hills, and in the valleys, and in all the coasts of the great sea over against Lebanon, the Hittite, and the Amorite, the Canaanite, the Perizzite, the Hivite, and the Jebusite, heard thereof; that they gathered themselves together, to fight with Joshua and with Israel, with one accord. . . .' "

He mouthed the words, unable to give them voice as he raised the derringer in both hands to his mouth. He had one bullet left. It was enough.

At the livery stable, the doctor awaited his escort.

TWENTY-FOUR

Blood Trail

They rode hard for almost ten miles in a wide swing north before Race felt safe enough to dismount and see to his cousin's injury. By that time Merle was dizzy from loss of blood and hugging his horse's neck to keep from pitching off. The saddle and the animal's right flank glistened glaring red from the leakage.

While Shirley and the squaw watched, Race cut open Merle's gory pants with a knife and used his kerchief to clear the wound. He cut away some more material, did some more cleaning, and laughed. His voice was high and nervous.

"Uncle John always said there wasn't nothing wrong with you that getting shot in the ass wouldn't cure," he said. "Reckon now we'll find out if he was right."

"Didn't get it in the ass." Merle sounded drunk. His words were slurred and hard to understand.

"That's where it come out, then. Same thing. Lean on me and we'll see to getting you down. I got doctoring to do."

"No, leave him there."

Race glared at Shirley, who had spoken. Woman Watching was readjusting the reins around the cripple's right stump. "You want him to bleed to death?"

"You want him to get shot again when that posse shows up and finds him still here?" countered Shirley. "You take him off that saddle, he'll stiffen up and you'll never get him back on."

"He's right," Merle said. "Do what you can for me here."

The squaw got down and helped clean the wound. Merle shuddered when they poured whiskey directly into the raw hole but didn't cry out.

"You shouldn't of shot the lawman, Merle." Race poked a strip torn from his shirt into each end of the wound to staunch the bleeding and tied a makeshift bandage around the thigh. "Now it's the knot if they get us."

"They won't get us."

His speech was almost normal. Race looked up at his cousin. Merle's eyebrows and moustache stood out startlingly against his pale face. But his eyes were clear and direct.

"They won't get us," he repeated.

"Goddamn Colorado weather," said George.

It was growing warmer. The snow seemed to recede before the Indian's eyes. What looked like hoof prints from a little distance turned out close up to be bare clumps of earth and grass around prairie dog holes, and the hoof prints themselves were losing shape so that when they did appear, he had to step down and study them before he could decide in which direction they were going. The pink drops of blood helped where they had landed on snow, but against the dead brown grass they were all but invisible. Such things had been much easier to see ten years ago.

Edwards pondered their surroundings. There were more buttes and the Continental Divide was taking definition to the west. "Chinooks blow in warm from Utah this time of year."

"Goddamn Utah weather, then. This way." George mounted and swung his horse's head northwest. The Mexicans followed morosely, Diego dwarfing the light pony he preferred to Paco's big American stud.

"They got to stop sometime," Edwards observed. "Wounded one's about bled out."

"Blood's like milk; you spill a pint and clean up two. If that bullet clipped an artery or anything else important, we'd have come across a corpse by now."

They rode for a time without conversing. The cloud cover was ragged and the sun slid in and out of view, warming the grassland and coaxing steam from the horses' withers. Finally Edwards spoke.

"Ain't you the least bit curious as to why the Cap'n turned the works over to you and stayed behind?"

"He's got a wounded man, or didn't you notice?" The Crow kept his eyes on the trail ahead.

"He's had wounded men before. He never elected hisself to stay with any of 'em."

"If I had a choice between slapping this saddle with my ass for the next God-knows-how-many days or warming it next to a campfire, I'd do the same."

"The hell you would. And neither would the Cap'n."

Reluctantly George looked at him. Edwards was the only man in the world capable of needling the Indian into doing something he didn't want to do. "All right. Why?"

"You know why," said the sharpshooter, grinning, and fell back.

George didn't press the point. Most of his life had been spent in the company of white men, and yet he was no closer to understanding them now than he had been the day he was kicked out of the mission school.

St. John kindled a fire out of the wood the Buckners had left behind and watched Rawlings turning his head this way and that in its orange glow. His breathing was rapid but strong, his pulse steady. He had stopped bleeding. His forehead was cool to the touch, but it was still too early for the fever of infection to set in if it was going to. St. John had his flask ready in case the Pinkerton awoke. His strict rule against drinking on manhunt didn't apply to medicinal use.

The sun was climbing. He wondered where Pierce was with that doctor. Already he regretted bowing to Edwards' wishes and sending the Sunday school teacher in his place. Testament was a killer, not an angel of mercy. But St. John had been too angry with himself for hurling the detective into danger to think straight, which was evidence enough that he was no longer the man for this work. Earp and Masterson had recognized the signs in themselves and retired East. Heck Thomas hadn't been heard from in a spell, and Bill Tilghman was riding a desk in a sheriff's office in Oklahoma. Only he, St. John, was still sitting posse. It made a man feel alone. He sipped at the flask for company. He sipped again, and then he stopped sipping and started drinking.

The container was empty by the time the doctor showed up, without Pierce.

TWENTY-FIVE

Magdalene's Children, II

Direct sunlight was cruel to Chloe Ziegler, plowing deep furrows between her nose and mouth and under her eyes faded to a glass blue, exposing the roughness of her complexion and the taut strings beneath her chin. Race, who knew what she was like between sheets, had never thought of her as an old woman, and in fact she was only ten years his senior, but in her plain blouse and skirt with the peeling paint of her country establishment at her back she looked like one of those frontier matrons he remembered from his Kansas childhood, worn out while still in their twenties from work and poverty and bears in the garden. Or maybe it was just him, and the fact that he had left his youth in the wash along with his provisions and camping equipment.

A few of her girls had started to come out with her when the mounted quartet came to a stop in front of the porch, but she had shooed them back inside and now they were watching from the doorway and through the curtains on the ground-floor windows. Merle, slumped over, half conscious, kept his seat with the support of Jim Shirley on one side and the Cherokee woman on the other. Their horses' sides heaved, slick with lather.

"I can't take any of you inside if you're being chased," Chloe told Race. Her head barely reached above his stirrup. "No one, not even Merle. You know that."

"I know. I don't want that." But he did, even though he knew it would be unwise to accept. The offer would have been enough to bring back some of his former confidence. "I need stores, enough for ten days. We had to leave most of what we had."

"Four people. You'll be needing a packhorse too."

He shook his head. "Slow us down. We'll get what we can in the saddlebags and carry what's left in our pockets. Small stuff—sardines and like that. No flour or bacon."

"You can get fresh horses down the road. Erik Meyer's ranch. But don't say it was me sent you." She called for one of the girls and sent her to the storehouse out back for the requested items.

Race said, "We can do with alcohol too, and stuff for bandages."

Chloe went inside. Waiting, Race revolved first one arm in its socket, then the other, working out the kinks. It was another holdover from his cowboy past, and anyway he'd pulled his right shoulder slightly swinging into the saddle that morning. He was conscious of the whores watching him. Then he glimpsed his reflection in one of the curtained windows and knew why. Haggard and unshaven, his eyes burning holes from lack of steady sleep, the face of a forty-year-old desperado glared back at him.

The girl who had gone out back returned dragging a clanking gunnysack filled with flat tins of fish in oil and cans of peas and beans and peaches. After the others had stuffed every available pouch and pocket, she brought the nearly empty bag to Race, who tied it around his saddle horn. The girl had tan eyes and natural red hair and a dust of freckles across the tops of her cheeks. Her gaze met his boldly and he sighed.

"No time, sweetheart."

"Get back in the house."

Chloe was back, carrying a bundle wrapped in a worn

towel. The redhead turned startled eyes on her and fled up the flagstone path to the door.

"Bitches in heat," muttered the madam, handing up the package. "Sometimes I think I'm running a kennel."

"Thanks, Chloe."

"We was out of alcohol so I put in a bottle of peroxide. Some of the ladies will just have to put up with black roots till I get to town."

He put it away in his saddle bag. "What do I owe you?"

"A thousand dollars."

He jumped. Startled, his horse snorted and fiddle-footed. He patted its neck.

"I could hold you up for a lot more, the risk I'm taking," she said. "You're lucky I like you. I could of sent you down the road in your long-handles or butted your face with the door when you came asking. Back in Leadville they'd of hit you over the head and trussed you up for the reward."

"Appears I'm swimming in good fortune." He got out his roll and peeled off a thousand. She accepted the bills without looking.

"I told you before to put them dime novels out of your head. If I had a heart of gold, someone would of cut it out and sold it for whiskey years ago."

The four turned back into the road. Merle swayed in his saddle but hung on. Bringing up the rear, her loose hat brim covering the back of her neck and much of her long black hair, Woman Watching resembled a mounted Buddha in occidental attire. Chloe returned to the house without looking back.

"I can't say I'm surprised," St. John observed, "though I never expected Testament to be the one to bust the cap on himself."

"Well, that's the rumor. I heard the shots, but I wasn't there to see it."

A gray-headed man with a full white beard and slightly protuberant eyes behind bifocals, the doctor was built along simian lines, with a tremendous chest, long powerful arms, but very thin short legs that gave him a deformed look overall. He had hopped down from the wagon seat with a quick, apelike movement and squatted with his black bag next to the wounded man after scarcely a grunt of greeting to St. John. While unbuttoning Rawlings' shirt to get at the injury he had described Midian Pierce's fate in terse phrases. Death didn't interest him nearly as much as the struggle to avoid it.

"What do you think, Doc?"

"I think you're drunk. I also think I don't like being called Doc." He probed the flesh around the wound with alcohol-soaked fingers. "My Christian name's Titus, but no one's called me that since my wife left me. I answer to Dr. Urquhart, or, if you prefer, just plain Doctor."

"All right then, Just Plain Doctor. What do you think?"

He cleaned and rebandaged the hole. "He's young and in good physical condition. He should survive the journey back to town. Beyond that I can't say."

"I'm paying you to say."

Urquhart glanced up at the old lawman, standing over him with legs spread, his fists down at his sides. "I'm a physician, not a clairvoyant. The bullet is very close to his heart. I won't know until I get inside what damage I might have to do to get it out."

"I always figured it was a doctor's job to repair other folks' damages, not make new ones."

"How can I explain it?" Urquhart sighed. "There is a network of major arteries leading to the heart. Picture a stone wedged between very thin glass vessels. I gather you're some kind of peace officer, from which I assume your hand is steady. Yet could you predict with certainty that you could remove that stone without rupturing any of the vessels that surround it?"

St. John exhaled. "I sure hope you doctor as good as you argue."

"We'll leave that judgment up to events." He spread the patient's shirt open the rest of the way and rolled gauze around his chest and up over his shoulder to fix the pad in place. While he was doing this he discovered the repair job to Rawlings' wrist, inspected it briefly, and nodded approval without removing it. "There's a mattress in the wagon box. Unroll it, will you? It should help absorb some of the bumps."

St. John complied, unstrapping the worn, striped pad and flattening it out against the boards. "How'd you find this place, anyway? Testament tell you?"

"I interrupted him while he was telling me. I'm the chief medical officer for this county. Two years ago I supervised the destruction of a hundred head of cattle near here during an anthrax breakout."

"You got a good head for directions for a doc. Doctor, excuse me."

"I should. I put myself through medical school hunting buffalo. Give me a hand getting him into the wagon."

They bore him carefully, Urquhart supporting the patient's torso in his great arms while St. John took his feet. Afterward they tucked the blanket around him and folded the edges under the mattress to keep him from rolling or sliding. Rawlings muttered something during the transfer but remained unconscious for the most part. Perspiration gleamed on his forehead, cheeks, and chin.

"Buffalo hider, huh?" St. John wiped his own face with his handkerchief. It wasn't that warm, but the Pinkerton was heavier than he had suspected. His heart pounded from the labor, skipping every third beat. He felt nauseated. "I wondered where you got that coat."

Urquhart was indeed wearing a buffalo coat, the tightly coiled hair covering his out-of-proportion frame from neck to ankles. "It's a badge of the profession, or was. When I was a boy in Denver, no doctor worth his shingle would be caught dead outside in the wintertime without one." He adjusted his hat, a shapeless brown slouch with a worn spot on the brim precisely where he put his fingers. "Are you sick?" he asked suddenly. St. John's face was gray.

"Just sore. I'm still getting broke back to saddle." He straightened his shoulders with an effort. His stomach was settling and his heartbeat was slowing, though it remained irregular. The handkerchief was soaked.

"It's your body." The doctor mounted to the driver's seat. "I assume you're accompanying me into town."

"Don't see as I got much choice. I'm unhorsed, or didn't you notice?"

The front door of Chloe Ziegler's house sprang open and struck the wall with a crash that reverberated throughout the building and scattered screws and washers from the smashed lock. The redhead who had brought stores to the Buckners screamed at the sight of a mean-faced Indian crossing the threshold. She was staring at him over the shoulder of a land developer in her embrace on the sofa.

The Indian was followed by two Mexicans, one small and rat-faced with blue scars on his shadowed cheeks, the other large and long-haired, both wearing crossed ammunition belts like bandits in photographs taken below the border. The big one saw the girl and grinned. His teeth were long and yellow like a horse's. There was black iron among them. She shuddered and held on tight to the developer.

Her companion gaped dumbly, his collar undone, his fleshy face smeared with rouge and powder. Then he disentangled himself and fumbled for the pistol in his back pocket. The Indian raised a gray steel revolver to within an inch of the developer's right eye and thumbed back the hammer loudly. The customer brought his hand forward empty and placed both palms on his thighs in plain sight.

The parlor was full of man-smells: gunpowder and horse and leather and sharp, stinging sweat. The developer's cologne fled before them like a maiden pursued by invading soldiers.

Chloe was standing in the curtained side entrance. The Indian halted in front of her, causing a near collision behind him.

"The door wasn't locked," she said firmly. "How long's it been since your last woman?"

"It's men we're after." For all his savage appearance, the Indian knew his way around English. "We've been following Race and Merle Buckner and Jim Shirley all day, and their trail leads right to your porch. Where are they?''

''They were here. I sent them away.''

''Took you long enough. The ground thawed out from under their mounts while they were outside.''

''It took some persuading.''

While they spoke, the small Mexican reached behind the developer and relieved him of his weapon. He laughed harshly. It was a .32-caliber one-shot derringer with a lady's pearl grip. Its owner flushed scarlet but kept silent.

''Nothing out back,'' reported yet a fourth man, appearing behind Chloe. He was tall and thin and wore spectacles. ''Buggy in the carriage house and a fistulowed nag in the corral. You ought to have a vet look at her, honey.'' He was addressing the madam. She made no reply and didn't even turn to face him.

''We'll have a look around,'' said the Indian.

''Where's your warrant?'' Irony edged her tone.

''We don't need one. We're private citizens. Hold still, there!'' The command was aimed at the fat developer, who had started to rise.

He settled back down next to the redhead. ''I was just leaving. You can't hold me here.'' His voice cracked on the last part.

''Watch him, Bill.'' The Indian took his gun off cock, belted it, and spoke in halting Spanish to the Mexicans, indicating the staircase. They nodded and started up the steps. Bill came in past Chloe and took a seat opposite the sofa. He removed his hat, smiling at the redhead. She smiled back tentatively. He was ash-blond and kind of handsome for a four-eyes, certainly easier to look at than the quivering mound of dough at her side.

The savage returned his attention to Chloe. His tone softened. ''I'd appreciate a tour of the ground floor if you're not busy.''

''I'm dressed, ain't I?'' She showed him her back and went through the doorway.

It was the lull before the busy hour. The cattle ranches were just shutting down for the day, and the nearest one was thirty minutes down the road by horse. George and the

woman interrupted only one whore at work. Her customer
exclaimed when he glanced back over his shoulder and saw
the Indian, but a quick motion of the Starr double-action
stopped him in the middle of reaching for a gun belt hanging on the bedpost. He returned to business as the door was
pulled shut with the visitors on the other side. The remain-
ing rooms were either vacant or occupied by women at
leisure in chemises or nothing at all. One was an Indian
girl with long black hair and a round, smooth face—Nav-
ajo, George guessed—who looked up in surprise over the
copy of *Harper's Weekly* she was reading on the bed, then
smiled at him archly. He closed that door with regret.

"Sun's going down," Chloe informed him. "Twenty
dollars buys an hour."

"Kind of steep, isn't it?" he asked. "And what makes
you think I wouldn't prefer a white woman, or is there a
rule against that here?"

"Men generally leave rules at the door when they come
here. Your choice, and if you still think it's steep after the
hour's up, I'll refund half."

His smile was stony. "You wouldn't be trying to buy
running time for your boyfriends now, would you?"

She threw back the expression like a mirror. "I got a
business to run. You'll be making camp in a half hour anyway. There's no moon tonight, and even an injun can't
track without light."

He considered. It was gray in the hall and growing chilly.
"Twenty, you said?"

Upstairs, the Menéndezes poked their heads through an
open door to find two rather hefty women, one about thirty,
the other barely out of her teens, conversing in bored tones
near the darkening window. The younger one was on the
bed in a nearly transparent dressing gown painting her toe-
nails violent red; her companion, dyed blond and wearing
a plain white shift with nothing on underneath, leaned
against the wall smoking a cheroot. They stopped talking
when the Mexicans appeared, but gave no evidence of
alarm.

Diego looked at Paco, whose grin came slower but

stayed just as long. They holstered their Colts and entered, swaggering like dons.

As the light in the parlor failed, so did Wild Bill Edwards' vision. He switched on a lamp and moved from his chair to the sofa to keep a closer watch on the developer, wedging himself between him and the redhead. She smelled of pink powder and scented soap. Neither of them noticed a few minutes later when the fat man picked up his hat and left, abandoning his derringer to the Mexicans.

TWENTY-SIX

Doctor's Orders

D r. Urquhart, looking more than ever like an orangutan in shirtsleeves and unbuttoned vest, emerged from his office into the waiting room wiping a fog of sweat from his bifocals with a wad of gauze. His collar was limp and drops of perspiration glistened at his temples like diamond dust in the light of the ceiling fixture; his hair was very thin there but grew profusely everywhere else, including the backs of his hands. St. John, who had been dozing on the bench, started and rose when the door opened. It was dark outside the window. The loud standard clock atop a glassed-in bookcase stuffed with leather-bound volumes read nine past ten.

"Hope you weren't lonely," Urquhart greeted, using the gauze to mop his fleshy palms. "Often my reception area is jammed even at this hour, but your late preacher friend seems to have taken care of that."

"What about Rawlings?"

"Oh, he'll live. He seems to be a remarkably resilient young man. He was shot once before, you know, in the left thigh. Several years ago, judging by the scar."

"I didn't know. He was in the war with Spain."

"So was I. Sailed with Dewey to Manila as a Naval

Reserve officer. Your friend's lucky I did. I learned most of what I know about separating lead from tissue once those Mausers started popping.'' He fished something out of a vest pocket and dropped it into St. John's palm. ''A souvenir.''

It was a lump of gray metal as big around as a man's finger, flattened somewhat by its contact with bone but retaining its conical shape.

''Give you some trouble, did it?'' asked the old lawman.

''Not at all. I spent most of the last four hours reading the *Police Gazette* and practicing my harmonica.''

St. John grinned weakly at the other's exasperation. ''Can I see him?''

''That's all you'd be doing, seeing him. He won't be conscious tonight, what with the ether and his blood loss. Nurse Wheeler is with him. You met her when we came in.''

St. John remembered the horse-faced woman in white cap and uniform, who had literally pushed him out of the consultation room when he had tried to follow Urquhart inside. ''You might say I ran into her.''

The doctor smiled faintly. ''Get some sleep. He might be up to visitors in the morning, but I can't say for sure. He really should be in the hospital. I would have taken him there if I didn't think the time lost making arrangements might be fatal. I can see already that this century is going to be tailor-made for clerks and bureaucrats.''

''What's the tariff, Doc? Dr. Urquhart,'' he corrected himself, mining out what was left of his bankroll from a coat pocket.

''We'll discuss it tomorrow. I'll hold on to Rawlings a few days for observation, maybe check him into the hospital, though he's comfortable enough for now on the cot in back. There's a fifty-fifty chance of infection, and if his blood pressure should go down, it means I missed some of the damage and will have to go back in. That's a remote possibility, but there are always a lot of ifs whenever metal and flesh meet. They weren't meant to, you know, despite your lawman's creed." He paused. "I just realized I don't know your name."

St. John told him. The physician nodded without showing surprise.

"I'd suspected as much. The city's alive with rumors about your mission, whatever it is. You've made a lot of work for my fellow practitioners over the years, Mr. St. John."

"I do what they pay me for, Dr. Urquhart. Same as you."

"There's a difference. In my line, when someone dies it means I've failed."

"Mine too." St. John massaged his left hand with his right.

Urquhart caught the gesture. "Is there something wrong with your hand?"

"Goes to sleep on me now and then."

"I see. Does this happen often?"

"Like I said, now and then." He put on his hat. The sweatband felt clammy against his forehead.

"Do you ever feel short of breath when you haven't exerted yourself?" Urquhart was all doctor now.

"From time to time. I'm fifty years old." He spoke sharply. The grilling irritated him. His heartbeat quickened slightly and became ragged.

"I'm sixty-four, and I've never had those symptoms. Bear with me one moment." He seized the other's left wrist in a grip best suited to a blacksmith's tongs and produced his watch, his broad flat thumb pressing the blue artery on the underside of the wrist.

"Your pulse seems erratic," he said, releasing his hold. "I'd like to listen to your heart, if you'll step into the consulting room."

St. John rubbed his forearm. There were purple marks where the doctor's fingers had dug in. "I don't hunt men I don't have paper for. You shouldn't doctor folks that don't come looking for it."

The physician was grave. "I wish you'd let me examine you. To be frank, I think you're a textbook candidate for a massive heart attack. It will only take a few minutes to confirm or confute my suspicion."

"I don't have a few minutes. I got to sleep fast and be riding come first light."

"My opinion, should you ask—"

"I won't."

"—is that you couldn't be in a profession more dangerous for your condition. You're walking dynamite. I'm not talking about a few weeks in the hospital. I'm talking about the rest of eternity in a hole six feet down."

"Save your bogey stories. I don't scare." St. John grasped the doorknob.

"You can say that now. See if you can when the time comes you can't fill your lungs no matter how hard you try, and your left arm starts tingling like a telephone bell. Because when that happens, even God won't be close enough to save you."

St. John hesitated, then opened the door. A draft of unheated air from the hallway chilled his face. "I'll stop by and settle with you on my way to the livery tomorrow."

"See that you do. I'd hate to have to sue your estate for it."

TWENTY-SEVEN

On the Scout

To the west, Wyoming's Red Wall reared the color of old blood in the emerging sun from brown and yellow grassland as flat as a bar top, the sandstone ridge looking like something picked up on another planet and hurled there just to spoil the planned effect. Still a day's ride off, it taunted the traveler, daring him to reach out and try to touch its grainy surface. The air was crisp and the spent breath of horse and man looked like etchings in brittle pewter. The grass crackled under the horses' shoes. They were six days out of Boulder and Chloe's place.

"How you doing, Merle?" asked Race.

Merle didn't answer. Riding beside him, Race's cousin was slumped so far forward the front tip of his hat brim touched his chest. His high sheepskin collar concealed the rest of his head and the gloved fingers around which his reins were twisted lay curled and lifeless atop his saddle horn. His other arm hung limp at his side, swaying with the animal's movements.

Alarmed, Race called his name. The hat brim rose slowly. Merle's face shone like polished marble. His moustache and whiskers looked painted on. Only his eyes seemed alive, holes scorched into a sheet with orange

sparks glowing in their centers. The hollows in his face
looked deep enough to hold water. He stared in his cousin's
direction for a long moment, obviously not seeing him, and
then his chin sank back down to his breast.

It had taken the trio to hoist him into his saddle at first
light, Shirley lending support with his back and shoulders
while Race got Merle's leg up and over and Woman
Watching held the skittish horse. The bleeding had stopped—
due more to the temperature than to the bandage—but the
flesh around the wound had turned an unhealthy red. Shirley
had recognized the first stage of gangrene but said it could be
just a minor infection. They had poured peroxide into it and
applied new dressing. This time Merle didn't flinch, another
bad sign.

Race drew rein to collect his bearings. Jim Shirley and
Woman followed suit, the squaw leaning over to catch
Merle's bit chain. Their only guide was a map of central
Wyoming Race had torn from a book about Butch Cassidy,
and he had already discovered it to be inaccurate. Now he
tugged off his gloves and got it out again, attempting to
relate its sketchy features to the surrounding terrain. Merle
knew this country, but Merle had all he could do to keep
his head up and his heels down, and Carroll, who had
crossed and recrossed it more times than even he could
have remembered, was gone—dead or in jail, and probably
dead. The information that spy had acquired could only
have come from Carroll, and Race knew well Carroll's de-
termination never to see bars again.

The map was worse than no help at all. It indicated
mountains where there was only prairie and barren desert
where springs fed clumps of maple and cottonwood that
hid the sky. It had likely been done up out of the imagi-
nation of some New York illustrator who had never been
west of Buffalo. *Yessir, Race Buckner, you're a regular
criminal genius, going on the scout in territory you don't
know from black Africa*. Well, he at least had the Red Wall.
Nebraska was for lying low, but Wyoming had all the best
places to run to in a hurry. He was refolding the dilapidated
sheet when Jim Shirley sidled over, steering with his knees.

"Hate to be the one to bring bad news," he said quietly, "but there's half a thousand miles 'twixt us and Canada, if that's where we're running, and Merle won't make the first two hundred."

"Ain't running to Canada."

Shirley nodded. He was as far from his last shave as were the Buckners and the skin was starting to peel off his cheeks and the end of his nose. "I never run with no gangs before I threw in with you, so be sure and stop me when I step out of bounds. Do I get some guesses, or are you just flat out going to tell me where it is I'm going to die?"

"Won't be no dying done on our side if this place turns out to be all they claim." Race fingered the dog-eared scrap of paper. "Your word you won't laugh?"

Shirley watched him, then nodded again. His eyes were as clear and guileless as a child's when his curiosity was aroused.

The gang leader opened the map and pointed a nail-bitten finger at the artist's conception of a gap in the great sandstone ridge that divided Wyoming into two equal parts, beside which was printed HOLE-IN-THE-WALL.

"I ain't laughing," Shirley told him, after a moment.

"Grab your pants!"

George withdrew his head from the darkened room, then remembered that Diego Menéndez was its occupant and stuck it back in.

"Agarra sus pantalones!" he repeated in Spanish.

Without waiting for a response he marched to the next room and fired the same command at Paco. Meanwhile Diego disentangled his limbs from those of the ripe blonde and reached for his boots. She stirred slightly, murmured something, and went back to snoring. There was too much frost on the window to see out, but he could tell it was still dark. The room was overheated and his threadbare long underwear felt clammy against his skin as he stepped into it.

He entered the hall buttoning his shirt and met Paco, fully dressed and looking alert despite his disheveled hair and scrubby beard. Youth. Diego accompanied him downstairs without a word.

A Negro handyman, with hair like yellowed cotton and a purple scar that followed the contours of his right cheek and made both of Paco's look modest by comparison, was laying a fire in the grate when they came into the parlor. There, George and Wild Bill Edwards were standing at a pedestal table they had cleared in order to place a pair of unmatched vases and other small items on top of it. Edwards moved them around like chesspieces.

"The Divide's here and they ain't going to get over it with a wounded man," he was saying. "Canada's too far. There's a half-dozen other ways they can go, but this one's the smartest. Bet my pearl-handled Colts on it."

"Sure you would, after all that sand Comanche Tom made you fire through them made pepper mills out of the barrels. What makes you so sure they won't just double back?"

"Would you, if you had a bunch of mean sons of bitches like us hot on your ass?"

"I say you're placing too much store in this wounded man of theirs. What if he dies or gets better? And who says they care one way or the other?"

"The wounded man is Merle Buckner." Edwards grinned as the Indian's face registered surprise. "You think I wasn't working last night? This lawman stuff gets in your blood."

"Whores lie just as much as the rest of us." George shrugged. "All right, let's just for now say it's Race's cousin who's hit. Who's to say the others won't outvote Race and leave Merle behind some rocks somewhere, to bleed out while they make a run for the Divide?"

"They're a small gang and they been riding together a spell. I know what that's like. It gets to be like family. They look out for each other."

"Family, hell. One of 'em's Indian, and a squaw to boot. I wasn't on furlough last night either," George added.

"I admit some folks ain't as tolerant as me. But it's my guess she looks after Shirley. He may be hell with that trick gun, but someone has to clean it and strap it on. That's their weak point, their closeness. Take out one member and the gang falls apart.''

"Say you're right. Where are they headed?''

"Where does any bandit head when he's in Wyoming and his pants are on fire?''

The Crow thought. "They wouldn't," he said then. "They know we'd expect it.''

"I been telling you and telling you they ain't got time for fancy. Damn it, will you listen to an outlaw explaining how an outlaw thinks? Remember what the Cap'n said about the marble in the fist?''

"They can buy protection anywhere. They have forty thousand dollars to spend.''

Diego perked up at that. He'd been following the gringos' argument in snatches, but the monetary amount came through loud and clear. He glanced at Paco, who looked bored. He hadn't understood.

Edwards said, "The railroad's offering five thousand for Race head up or feet first. Anyone he could buy protection from would put holes in him and the others for the reward and pick the forty off their bodies. Folks protected Jesse and Frank out of the Christianity in their souls, but Jesse's been dead a long time and folding money has a nasty crackle.''

"I wish St. John were here," George said. "His brain has eyes.''

"So has a potato, but we ain't got one of those neither.''

The Indian scowled down at the table. "Which one's the Red Wall, the vase or the soup tureen?''

Diego had stopped listening. He was busy mentally converting forty thousand dollars into pesos.

A naked bulb trickled white light down the narrow rubber-runnered staircase that led from Dr. Urquhart's office to the street. Shadows crouched in the corners and a draft of cold air found its way up inside St. John's pantlegs as he descended, the old wood complaining under his weight so early in the morning. That weight was lighter by thirty dollars now in the doctor's possession for the past and future care and feeding of Emmett Force Rawlings.

The Pinkerton had been asleep when St. John looked in on him, but when the chain was pulled on the overhead fixture Rawlings' eyes had blinked open long enough to recognize the old lawman, then closed as something that looked like a faint smile tugged at the corners of his mouth. That alone was worth more than the thirty. But St. John's mood was heavy again as he opened the door and stepped outside. It always was at that time of day, when the sun was still absent and the streets were empty, the corner lamps glowing for no one but him. Today it was worse. It hadn't always been this way. He remembered waking up warm under a thick counterpane with the icy bedroom air on his face and his wife's hand touching his shoulder, and the sensation of physical love in the morning. The civilized world was in bed with a warm woman at this hour, not getting set to mount an animal already snorting under the burden of foodstuffs and ride out over frozen ground after men with guns. Not at fifty years old, with rheumatism in the legs and a tired heart.

The horse was a shaggy black, short-coupled and unmarked, the way he preferred them. It was the one Pierce had chosen for him. Testing the cinch, St. John thought of the little Sunday school teacher stretched out naked on the table in the undertaker's back room. Dead, he had looked tinier than the posse chief remembered. The .41 slug had had just enough power to exit through the top of his skull after passing through his brain, jellying his gray-streaked hair. The undertaker said it had come rolling out when the hat was removed. St. John had paid ten dollars for a proper headboard and left the corpse to the expert's care. On his way out he had passed two rooms in which lay Fred Dieterle and the hotel detective, dress-suited in boxes mounded with flowers to cover the smell of the embalming fluid, Dieterle's closed for shipment to his home in Nebraska. No such niceties for their killer; just plain unlined wood and a hole in Strangers' Corner. The old lawman wondered what had lain between Pierce and the Nebraskan. There was a young girl mixed up in it somewhere, sure enough.

Breathing was like inhaling needles. St. John grasped his saddle horn, made a false start, and straddled on the second try. He was glad none of the others had been around to see that. None of them would have commented on his failure, but the spore of doubt would have spread among them like pollen in a high wind. That was the part of the job that wearied him the most, the inability to react naturally in the face of difficulty. Like a clown with a painted-on face in the circus. He had spent most of his life setting an example for his men and the effort had cost him twenty years. He felt seventy.

The frozen-stiff macadam rang under his horse's iron shoes, the only set that seemed to be working in all of Denver at that hour. The noise echoed off the darkened buildings. Behind him, the sun sent a pale scout to warm the sky before it left its bed below the earth's curvature, but the sky was blue and almost as cold as the night itself. A blind worm of pain so deep it never saw the light stirred in St. John's right hip joint and began the long crawl down the marrow to his knee.

TWENTY-EIGHT

The Hole

They reached the shale-cluttered slope at the base of the wall late in the day. Ringed in on three sides by stacked buttes, the dry valley graded upward in a semicircle like a ruined coliseum, beyond which the sandstone ridge, more brown than scarlet now that they were almost up to it, stretched for fifty miles as straight as a guitar string. Its top was as even as a board fence but for a perfect triangular notch like a rifle sight where the pass reached its summit. This was the infamous Hole-in-the-Wall, from which a single rifleman, given enough ammunition, could hold a platoon of cavalry in check for a month. So legend had it.

"I was expecting something more like a proper hole," Shirley commented. They had dismounted beyond range of the rocks and were helping Merle down, Woman Watching grasping the wounded man by his lapels and heaving. She was as strong as most men.

"Me too," grunted Race. "But then nothing's turned out like I expected since I quit punching cows."

"Ever knock one down?" Merle had rallied somewhat. Repeated flushing of his wound had arrested the infection and he was conscious most of the time, though he required support while his bed was prepared. His face was still very white.

"Shut up and get better," Race said.

His cousin chuckled weakly. They wrapped him in blankets and left him sitting on the ground while Race unburdened the mounts and the squaw foraged for kindling. The buffalo chips that made such a fine blue flame in the old days were all gone now, as were the buffalo themselves. Even their bones were gone, to fine china and the sugar refineries back East. The men who had killed them were dead or home by the fire, gumming soft bland food and complaining about the chalk in their joints.

"Feel it, Jim?" Race dumped the last of the saddles onto the ground, bare of snow thanks to the sheltering buttes. "There's ghosts in this here valley."

"You see one, ask him how my hands are doing." Shirley whistled through his teeth at the Cherokee, who dropped the wood she had gathered to place a cheroot in his mouth and set fire to it. Then she returned to her labors.

"Not real ghosts. I mean history. Butch and the Kid and Elzy Lay and Harvey Logan and the Tall Texan and the rest. They all came through here regular, which is why they call this the Outlaw Trail instead of the Deadwood stage route, which is what it was. We're in famous company."

"They're all dead or in hiding. Company like that I can do without."

Race sighed. "You know what your trouble is, Jim? You got no romance in your soul."

"Guess I had it blasted out of me." The cripple blew smoke. It drifted up out of sight and was shredded by the wind off the rocks.

Woman Watching built a good Indian fire scarcely larger than a man's hand ("white man make fire big, sit back, no good. Indian make fire small, stay close, get warm"), next to which was placed a large can of beans on a shard of shale. When it was sizzling she wrapped a cloth around it and passed it among the fugitives with a spoon in it, feeding Shirley herself, until it was empty. Then the last of Race's bottles made the rounds. When it got to Merle he lifted it in both hands, spilling more down his chin than he swallowed. A high flush stained his pale cheeks like blood on a fish's belly. The squaw accepted the bottle and started to raise it to Shirley's lips, but he took it between his stumps and helped himself to a long draft. Race drank last and started the operation all over again.

"Woman can have some too if she wants," he told Shirley. "This ain't downtown."

"She don't drink."

Merle laughed feebly. "Injun don't drink's like a pump without washers."

"That's what her husband thought till a bunch of vigilantes took him from a saloon in Guthrie and strung him to a telegraph pole. He was too drunk to fight back."

"They lynched him for drinking?" In the firelight Race's eyes were big.

"They figured he put it to someone's daughter or niece or something. White woman."

"Did he?"

"Hell, I don't know. Thing is, neither did they."

Woman Watching said nothing, but her bright black eyes darted between Race and the cripple, understanding. She passed the bottle to Shirley, who held it out to the younger Buckner in his stumps without partaking. Race was too busy watching the flames to accept it. Shirley lowered the vessel to the ground between them.

"Hell of a thing to do to a man, run a rope around his neck and stretch it," Race said.

"Depends on who does it." Merle huddled deeper into his blanket. It was dark out now, and though the fire roasted their faces their backs were growing cold. "I seen a fellow take the drop in Helena. Hangman snugged the knot up under his left ear so that when they opened the trap his neck snapped like a dry cornstalk. Sounded like a pistol shot. He didn't kick but a damn little. There's worse ways to die."

"Not for me," said Race. "I'd take a bullet in the gut and go slow before I'd let them do that to me."

"Wasn't no snap when they hung the injun, Woman

says," put in Shirley. "He strangled slow. His face turned black and his pants fell down and he disgraced himself." He raised the bottle, drank.

The squaw fed the fire.

"You figure you killed that lawman at the wash?" Race asked Merle finally.

"I sure as hell tried." He drew his blanket tighter.

"You said that before."

"Meant it both times."

"I was sort of counting on us not having to do that. Ever."

"He was going to do it to us," Merle argued. "That posse wasn't there to bring us fresh horses. What the hell was I supposed to do, kiss him?" His flush deepened.

"Yeah, killing him did us a lot more good."

"He killed Carroll, for chrissake!"

"We don't know that."

"It's done," Shirley said calmly. "So shut up."

Race, who had started to rise, sank back down onto his blanket. His cousin was shivering in spite of the sweat glistening on his face. The squaw threw her own blanket around his shoulders on top of his. He reached across for the bottle and splashed some of its contents down his throat, gulping audibly. His hands shook. "Damn it, I'm bleeding again."

Shirley signaled to Woman Watching, who got up and went for the bandages and peroxide. The cold was strengthening. As she worked on Merle, the others watched the flames and drank and listened to the wind humming among the rocks as through a gallows.

At dawn they helped Merle into his saddle and began the long climb to the pass. Ice glittered treacherously between the rocks that paved the ascent, slowing their progress. The day was half gone when white smoke blossomed in the high notch and a fragment of shale in Race's path split with a loud pop. The report followed.

.   •   •   •

Dawn stole into Chloe Ziegler's room, igniting dust motes and limning her profile, so like a man's, against the pillow and the floral-print wallpaper next to the bed. St. John lay beside her in that blissful half-world between waking and rising. His heart was functioning normally and for once his rheumatism wasn't bothering him. It was there—it never left entirely—but he had learned to welcome the remission of pain as he had once welcomed its absence. She kept the room cold, bringing memories of his wife before things went wrong.

Chloe stirred and mined a bare, slightly sinewy arm out from under the spread to fling across his chest. She wore a white cotton nightgown fastened at the shoulders. From the base of her neck to her hairline and from the break of her wrist to her fingertips her skin was dark, shades darker than her arms and bosom. St. John remembered that her chest and backside were flat and that the flesh of her thighs concealed muscles that gripped like taut cables. She was the kind of woman he used to see a lot of on the frontier before the railroads flooded it with Gibson girls.

"You plow like a farmer," she said sleepily.

He was holding her hand, stroking the fine ridge of callus at the base of her fingers. "That good or bad?"

"Um."

"You better answer. I'm vain as a stallion." Playfully he pried her fingers apart.

She withdrew her hand. "Well, it beats those thirty-second wonders from the Bar G."

"How do I compare with Race Buckner?"

She turned over onto her back. She was wide awake now, staring at the seam where the wall and ceiling met. She made no answer.

"There's ways and ways to track a man," he explained. "Most read sign, but I was never good at that. I generally favor planting my feet where he's planted his and seeing what comes of it. If he stayed in a hotel overnight, I try to get the same room, sleep in the bed he slept in. If he ate in a restaurant, I order what he did. I drink his brand of whiskey, smoke his cigars, and if he's a reading man, I read the books and newspapers he left behind. Judge Parker smiled when I told him that. He called me Swami Ike when we were alone. But by the time the Congress closed down his court and I ran up eighty-six arrests on a hundred and two warrants, he wasn't smiling anymore. When he was sick, just before he died, he called me in and said, 'Ike, if I had nine more men like you, I'd have disbanded the court myself, because there wouldn't be anyone left to arrest.' '' He fell silent, remembering the strict Ohioan.

"And humping the same whore is purely in the line of duty." Chloe spoke flatly.

"Not purely," he said, coming out of his reverie. "Man's got to cut the bear loose from time to time or bust."

"I ought to charge you a crystal-ball fee on top of the usual." She pounded her pillow, bunched it behind her back, and sat up. "Well, what did you find out?"

"Nothing," he confessed. "I clean forgot all about the Buckners."

There was no immediate response. Then he felt a tremor in the mattress and realized she was stifling laughter. He grinned shamefacedly. Propping himself up on one elbow, he fumbled a cigar and a box of matches out of his coat hanging on the back of the chair beside the bed. Gray smoke uncoiled toward the east window.

"I know some men who voted for you for Congress," she said. "They were on their way to Missouri. Democrats was paying fifty dollars a vote plus traveling expenses."

"No wonder I lost out. Republicans were paying a hundred."

"That why you went back to marshaling?"

"I'm used to eating. Can't seem to buck the habit."

She said, "I get a lot of politicians. Carpetbaggers from back East and the grass-roots fellows that grew up on potato farms and took mail-order courses to get to be lawyers. You ain't like them. You run off at the mouth same as them but you don't talk about the same things. You're better off shed of them."

"Bull can't put on pants and be a man, that it?"

"Who said they was men?" She paused. "I suppose when you catch up with Race you'll kill him."

"Not if there's a better way."

"I hear that a lot from lawmen. There never is, when the reward's the same dead as alive. Man with the dollar sign on his head always gets shot resisting arrest or trying to escape. That way he don't have to be fed or tied up on the way back."

"I'd take the trouble."

"Sure you would. You ain't running for office now. Stop trying to get my vote."

He said, "The edge wore off killing years ago. I never did enjoy it, but I got to where it didn't make my guts boil anymore, which is about as bad. Yesterday I buried a man who liked it. He got to liking it so much he wound up doing it to himself."

"Race wouldn't kill a yellow dog."

"I got a man in Denver might not agree. Doc there dug a Buckner bullet out of his chest."

"Race wouldn't do that unless his back was to the wall," she insisted, "and maybe not even then. I'd believe it of Merle or Jim Shirley before I'd believe it of him."

St. John smoked. The sun was a gaping wound over Nebraska.

She said, "Can you control that posse of yours?" She had told him about George's visit.

"Don't let the Crow's nasty look throw you," he said. "He takes orders like Moses on the mountain. Wild Bill's the same."

"What about the Mexicans? I trust them like a bent six-shooter."

"You can count on a Mexican as long as you keep paying him."

"Or until someone else pays him better."

He let that slide.

"How'd you find out Race ever came here?" she asked then. "The injun send you a telegram?"

He shook his head. "I asked around. Outlaw on the scout can always count on help from a house of ill fame. You

get talked about a lot.'' He pulled aside the spread and
swung his bare feet to the iron-cold floor, reaching for his
long johns. Feeling her eyes on him, he sucked in his stomach as he pulled them on. ''You're mighty damn curious
for a woman in your line.''

"I'm writing a book. You're Chapter Twelve.''
She sounded serious.

"You're surrounded! Ditch the iron!''
The response was slow in coming. George's command
banged among the rocks, gradually losing shape until it
staggered out into the empty prairie and died.

After the Indian's shot from the cover of the notch, the
man riding in front below had either flung himself or been
thrown from his saddle as the mount reared, coming down
hard on stiff forelegs and arching its back. He rolled when
he struck ground and ended up behind a pile of rubble with
grass growing out of the spaces between the rocks. The
others had followed his lead, one of them—Merle, George
guessed—lowering himself more carefully and favoring
one leg as he scrambled for the shelter of an indentation in
the cliff to his right, carrying his rifle. The other two remained together as they fastened themselves to the opposite
wall of the pass. They'd be Jim Shirley and the Cherokee
woman.

A bullet spanged off stone twenty feet to George's left.
He stayed put behind his rock.

"You got 'er, friend!'' Merle shouted. ''Piece at a
time!''

The older Buckner's voice sounded normal; his echo betrayed the labored pause between sentences. George
knocked a piece off the rock Merle was hiding behind. The
high thin twang of the ricochet went on forever.

He wondered how long he could keep them pinned down.
If the rest of the posse had started at first light from their
last camp as planned, he could expect them in three or four
hours. He wished his marksmanship were as good as Wild
Bill's, and given his choice he would have sent Edwards
in his place, but if the hard ride through the night was too

dangerous for the whole group to attempt, it was certainly so for the half-blind former train robber. The problem was that George had no ammunition for the Winchester beyond what was in the magazine and in his pockets. He had sacrificed his saddlebags for the sake of speed. Thanks to Edwards' nearly photographic memory of the country, he had managed to beat the Buckners to the Hole just as the sky was turning gray. Without the former's detailed word map he would still be wandering the grasslands, because this was unfamiliar territory for a Crow born and reared in the Nations.

A movement behind the grass-grown rubble attracted his attention. Race—yes, it would be Race—was motioning with one hand, attempting to lure his skittish mount near enough to get his hands on the rifle in the saddle scabbard. George chucked one at its feet to frighten it off. The bullet squealed off stone, the horse screamed and folded down onto its side, kicking.

"Damn!" He fired three more times as Race lunged from behind shelter and came down on the other side of the fallen animal, clutching and sliding the long-barreled rifle out of leather. Two of the shots kicked up dirt. The third struck the horse with a ripe thump. Its head went down and it stopped kicking.

The Indian had practically dropped the rifle in Race's lap.

Zzzeeeooo! Lead buzzed past George's ear while he was reloading. It sounded like an enraged wasp. He had heard that noise once before, when a Spanish sharpshooter Comanche Tom had imported from Mallorca had been showing off between performances and fired his Mauser at a tent pole near George, parting it and sending the rope swinging. There was no mistaking that high-powered scream. The Crow was outgunned.

Zzzeeeooo! Zzzeeeooo! He crouched lower, thumbing fresh cartridges into the slot with shaking hands. In the east the sun was nailed in position as securely as he was nailed to that spot. "Indian luck," he muttered, leveling his carbine across the rock and sighting down the slope.

TWENTY-NINE

Shirley

The pebble was wedged so tightly between the shoe and the hoof that Wild Bill Edwards had to pare away some of the horny growth with his knife and pry with both hands, holding the gray's fetlock between his knees. He felt a momentary surge of triumph when it popped free, but the emotion quickly changed to disgust when he saw that the hoof was split.

He released it and straightened. The horse touched down the right forefoot gingerly, snorted, and lifted it again. Edwards scanned the vast empty grassland as if hoping to conjure up a blacksmith and forge. The Mexicans watched him patiently from their saddles, their black Yaqui eyes flat and impenetrable. Not a word had passed between them and their new leader since George's withdrawal. Edwards spoke no Spanish and communicated when necessary with hand signals. He uncorked one now, indicating for them to step down and walk their animals. They had passed a ranch five miles back where a fresh mount might be obtained. Would be obtained, he corrected himself. He was a lawman now, which carried certain privileges not unlike those he had enjoyed as an outlaw.

The sky was a scraped blue against which the sun yellowed and rose, drawing brilliant winking lights out of the new snow not yet twelve hours old. Edwards kept his eyes down, but they began aching after only a few minutes, and by the time the trio came within sight of the ranch house and corral, his head was hammering. He was blinded by darkness and agonized by bright light. That gray half-world between the sun and the stars had become his home, one that grew narrower daily. The future was a nightmare of blackness and dependence. He tried not to think of it, and because he tried, he thought of it most of the time. But he had his guns, and a man didn't need eyes to find his own head in the dark.

He located the owner of the spread leaning on his elbows on the corral fence, a lean small gray man with a moustache that tickled his ears and a bony face weathered to match his Stetson and cowhide coat. A pair of young cowpokes stood on the front porch at lazy attention, watching the strangers closely. The rancher kept his eyes on the horses in the corral while Edwards explained his predicament, then splattered tobacco juice at a fence post already glazed with brown liquid and said he had none to spare. Edwards replied that he was sorry it had to be this way and drew on him. The cowpokes were still going for their belt guns when the Mexicans unlimbered their big Colts. A rifle barrel nosed through an open window on the ground floor of the house. Diego snapped off a quick one that splintered the sill. The rifle hit the porch with a clatter and its owner, another young hand, with white-blond hair and a coppery sprouting on his upper lip, threw up his hands. The Menéndezes kept the peace while Edwards entered the corral and transferred his gear from the gray to a white-stockinged roan.

As the trio left, their late benefactors scrambling to rescue their weapons from the water trough in front of the house, it occurred to Edwards that except for the scribbled receipt he had put in the rancher's breast pocket, he was doing pretty much the same things in the name of the law that he had been sent to prison for the first time.

•   •   •

Back in the Nations, Irons St. John had enjoyed the reputation of being the man to get the most good out of a horse short of killing it, and he brought that long-forgotten talent into play now. Ride ten miles, walk five. A man could make a hundred miles a day that way easy, and still have enough horseflesh left to get him out of a tight spot. He didn't waste time studying the ground or examining broken blades of grass. His tracking skills had never compared with his riding and shooting, and anyway he knew where he was going.

The key to his manhunting success—a secret he kept to himself—was planning. Preparation was all, and that included poring over all the maps of the territory he was likely to cover during a hunt again and again, branding the details on his memory until he could find his way through it in the dark. Once he had made certain that the Buckners had crossed into Wyoming there was no doubt as to their eventual destination. Even as the thought occurred to him, the various routes by which a rider might reach the Hole-in-the-Wall country sprang to mind in the form of those dotted lines and arrows cartographers found so useful. For all of St. John's much-vaunted sixth sense, it was less than no help at all without sound groundwork.

His heart felt fine. Action was his tonic. It was during the quiet periods, when he lost his seat astride his own destiny, that he suffered. With Rawlings on the mend and his quarry's scent in his nostrils his late depression seemed like something that had befallen someone else. He could kick himself with spurs on every time he thought about how close he had come to turning down the Pinkerton's offer back in Kansas City. His backside was fit to the saddle, not a stuffed leather chair behind a big desk in some office in Washington. Wolves don't die dogs.

He slowed from a canter to a trot. He'd been outrunning his wind and had to alter his pace to breathe. That was all he had to be concerned about at this time in his life, shortness of breath and stiff joints. Doctors were always trying to scare folks. The wise man learned to adjust himself to his new limits, he thought, sucking in great lungfuls of sweet cold air.

• • •

There was only one thing James Blaine Shirley hated more than dependence and that was helplessness.

The day he had awakened in the Cuban field hospital and saw the bandaged stumps where his hands had been, he had smashed a glass cabinet and was fumbling a long, glittering shard between them to slash his throat with when the orderlies had come in. They had wrestled him back into bed, two of them struggling to hold him down while a third fixed the retaining straps in place. After that he had refused to eat. Then a two-hundred-pound corporal had sat on his chest, pinched his nose in one hand, and when the patient opened his mouth to breathe, spooned soup down his throat. Shirley's fast ended in the face of a threat to repeat the procedure every time he turned down a meal.

Stateside, the straps were eventually dispensed with. He resigned himself to being cared for, to the extent that he would do nothing for himself, including wipe his backside. This went on for twelve weeks, at the end of which a doctor who was also a full colonel strode into the ward, grasped the patient's iron bedstead in one corded hand, and pitched its occupant out onto the floor, announcing in a high, thin bray that the taxpayers of the United States had not financed a war against Spanish imperialism to install an oriental potentate in their own midst. Shirley's discharge followed soon after, following an awards ceremony at which President McKinley presented him personally with the Medal of Honor.

The event shamed its recipient, still stinging from the colonel's harsh words. He decided that since it was his hands that were lost and not his feet, he should learn to stand on them. But jobs were scarce for handless veterans. The war was forgotten in less time than it had taken to win, and the Industrial Revolution required workers with all their limbs who could handle tools and machinery. His wound pension struggled for a time against twentieth-century prosperity and inflation, then gave up. He had no family to whom he could turn for support. He tried to sell his story to a journalist he met in a Brooklyn bar, but the newspaperman told him his editor had a file on the war with Spain thick enough to fill his columns for the next five years had he wanted to do so, which he didn't. Finally Shirley scraped together enough cash to head West, like so many others who had gone before him in search of opportunity. The opportunity was there, without doubt, but it was slippery and had to be grasped with two hands—if you had them— or it was gone.

He bought his double-action Colt from a gunsmith in McAlester, Oklahoma Territory, and together they worked out the knotty problem of how to operate it without fingers. The streamlining and the straps were Shirley's idea. The gunsmith suggested that a coin be fused to the exposed trigger for easy access with his other stump. Shirley provided the gold piece, a good-luck charm from the days when he could expect good luck occasionally. Patiently he taught himself to load and unload the weapon by taking the bullets between his teeth, and spent day after day practicing his marksmanship in the Ouachita Mountains until the gun took the place of the longest index finger a man ever had, returning to the gunsmith's shop every night for cleaning and oiling.

That was the part he had resented, his dependence on another for the delicate work. He trusted no one else, which put him on a short tether with McAlester at the center. He had been drunk in a canvas-and-clapboard saloon on the edge of town, grumbling to himself over this state of affairs for the thousandth time, when the tinhorn came in with his Cherokee mistress in tow, the former already less lucid than Shirley, offering the woman in a loud voice to anyone in the place who would stand him to a drink. Shirley was the only taker. Next morning, sober and hung over, the gambler came to the cripple's campsite looking to take her back. When Shirley refused, his visitor produced a revolver and Shirley blew daylight through him with the Colt.

The tinhorn was a stranger to the area. No charges were pressed, on the condition that his killer agreed to leave town and never come back. He did, accompanied by Woman

Watching. She took quickly to firearms maintenance and he no longer needed the gunsmith.

Good fortune had smiled on his first experience with armed robbery. He walked into a Guthrie emporium just as the proprietor was getting ready to take his day's proceeds to the bank, stuck his gun in the merchant's face, and walked out with six hundred dollars and change in a locked bag under his arm. This stake got him to Pueblo, Colorado, where he robbed his first bank—an adobe hole with an old green safe inherited from Wells Fargo for a vault—making off with less than two hundred because the bank was about to fold. While escaping he literally ran into Race Buckner, who was on his way in to stick up the same establishment. At that point the bank's owner, an old cattleman's clerk who had served part of a term as interim sheriff in another county, came to the door and aimed a revolver at Shirley's back. Race saw him first and drew his Remington, firing and shattering the threshold at the banker's feet. The man's gun went down, his hands went up, and the two desperadoes fled together after relieving him of his watch and gold ring. Woman Watching followed. Merle Buckner's subsequent release from prison swelled the gang to four and they had been together ever since.

Now Shirley cursed the mysterious rifleman at the top of the pass. He had never suffered from claustrophobia, but the symptoms were identical, especially in his case because his boundaries at the best of times were narrow. This was worse than the invisible rope that had bound him to the gunsmith in McAlester. Each time he attempted to move along or away from the rock wall, the rifle sneezed smoke, lead twanged off stone near his head or chugged into the gravel at his feet. Even more frustrating was the knowledge that he and his companions were merely objects of sport; the sniper wasn't out to kill anyone or they'd all be feeding buzzards by now.

Jim Shirley rested his gun arm at his side, feeling more like a cripple than he had since leaving the military hospital in Florida.

•　•　•

For the hundredth time George checked the sun's position, determining for perhaps the tenth time that at least two hours had elapsed since his opening shot. December wind whistled through the pass and up under his coat and shirt. His back was numb under his flannels, both from cold and from standing in the same attitude for too long. Like everyone else of his generation he had a bad back. He envisioned his first week back in civilization lying on his stomach in a hotel bed under a warm moist towel, provided he held out until the last member of the gang was in custody and he collected his pay from St. John. Otherwise it would be a long cold ride East in a baggage car and agony on horseback in Comanche Tom's show. No, not Tom's. He had effectively closed the door on that option when he "scalped" the old fraud in front of a tentful of his fans. Another show then, if one would have him. But the season was over, which meant a long dry spell until spring. He decided that he didn't care. That moment under the lights outside Seminole had been worth it.

He wrenched his thoughts back to the job at hand, just in time to kick up dirt behind Merle as the fugitive was attempting to make his way back down the pass. So they had figured out that they weren't surrounded after all. Well, he hadn't expected the bluff to last any longer than it took to knock the edge off that dangerous panicky moment when a hunted animal is surprised in its natural habitat. George wished that Wild Bill and the Mexicans would hurry.

The earth at his feet glittered with spent brass cartridges. He reloaded, instinctively counting with his fingers those that remained in his last pocket. Thirteen rounds, one less than two full loads. He had fired around twice. Seven per hour. At this rate he had about two hours left, by which time the others should have arrived.

The cripple hugging the right wall dropped his gun arm suddenly, startling the Indian into jerking the trigger. He hit the wall just short of Shirley's face. Shirley pulled back, grit in his eyes. Woman Watching stepped into the open, grasping him by the shoulders to force him into cover.

George drew a bead on a grassy clump near her right moccasin. Keeping house.

He was squeezing the trigger when the sun passed from behind a rogue cloud, flashing off the carbine's front sight. His arm jumped involuntarily, elevating the muzzle a fraction of an inch. Flame squirted. Woman Watching spun and fell and didn't get up.

Shirley was still digging dirt out of his eyes when the bullet struck the squaw. The report all but drowned out her gasp, and then there was a sound that reminded him of the army and baled uniforms landing on the floor of the quartermaster's shack. Desperately he dragged his sleeve across his eyes. The Cherokee lay on her face at his feet.

He knew she was dead. He'd seen too many corpses in similar positions to believe otherwise. At first he didn't know how he felt about it. Then something inside him broke, something that had been a long time mending after his awakening in the field hospital in Cuba. He shoved back the sleeve on his gun arm with the other stump.

"Jim!" Race was shouting from the cover of his slain horse. "Jim, don't!"

Shirley didn't hear him. There was a roaring in his ears and his face felt hot. His eyes were still watering, blurring the rocks and spindly tree growth. They looked like the steaming jungle terrain around Santiago. The noise of the rifle, still echoing in the distance, resembled the crackling of Spanish Mausers. He stepped away from the wall, raising the Colt.

"Jim!"

He fired three times and was swinging his other stump forward for a fourth pull when another puff of smoke erupted at the top of the pass.

George thought he was having hallucinations. His revulsion over the result of his muffed shot was just taking hold when the cripple abandoned cover, presenting a clear target against the valley behind him as he brought up his short-ranged weapon. The Indian fancied he could hear the bullets plopping to the ground far short of his position. Well, it wasn't his decision to make. He rubbed the glare off the front sight with a thumb and aimed high, compensating for slope and distance. The Winchester's butt pushed at his shoulder when the trigger was depressed.

A fist slammed into Shirley high on his torso, snapping his collarbone in two and emptying his lungs with a *whoosh*. Another blow followed as his shoulder struck the rock wall. He tried to brace himself against it, but started sliding. He gave up trying halfway down. He died in Cuba, his gun stump stretched out toward Woman Watching as if reaching to grasp a cheap bronze star in fingers long since buried and gone to bones on an island ninety miles off Key West.

THIRTY

St. John

As he pushed his horse nearer its limit, Irons St. John was agonizingly conscious of time passed and opportunity lost. The sun was almost gone, dragging down colorful streamers like bunting at a Democratic Party rally, and he was just approaching the slope that led up to the Hole. The black's side heaved. Its coat was so streaked with white lather it looked from a distance like a cow pony. Grotesque shadows made a moonscape of the valley, emphasizing the eerie silence.

He had passed a stray horse two miles back, a big bay saddled and bridled and loaded with gear, but it kept sidling away from him and he had finally given up trying to overtake it. It was a strange animal and he didn't recognize the gear. If it belonged to one of the Buckners, the old lawman had missed some excitement. The trail he had taken from there had been used within the day. The confusion of horseshoe tracks baffled his limited powers to read sign.

His mount almost stepped on the carcass lying in shadow. It stumbled back whistling. St. John held his seat. He was pondering the dead horse when a voice hailed him.

"Speak up or die! This here's the law talking!"

The echoes in the valley mocked St. John's inability to

place the source of the challenge, but he knew it had to have come from the summit. "Whoa up, Wild Bill," he called back. "Shoot me, you don't get paid."

The silence crept back in for a beat. Then the man in the Hole invited him up. St. John dismounted, leading the nervous black around the cold horsemeat.

Two smaller bundles shared the darkness at the base of the left wall. St. John put on his glasses to examine them. One was a young Indian woman, shot through the heart. The other was a man with no hands and a hole in his upper chest. The earth around him was soaked deep with blood. The bullet had severed a major artery. St. John returned the spectacles to their case in his breast pocket and resumed climbing. His heart was bounding off his breastbone. Missing every fourth beat. He walked through the mist of his own labored breathing.

Edwards was standing at the top holding his rifle in one hand. His eyes met St. John's through his thick corrective lenses, then slid down and to his left. An arm in a heavy coat sleeve hung over the top of a tall boulder. George's Winchester lay on the ground at its base.

"Ran out of ammunition," said Edwards. "He was fixing to hold 'em down till we got here. He done it as long as he could." His voice broke on the last part.

St. John didn't move. "What about the Mexicans?"

"Behind you."

He turned to look. Paco and Diego were incongruous shadows in the thickening dusk halfway down the slope. They had been watching him from behind the rocks and brush that hugged the walls of the pass. They were holding their Mexican Winchesters.

St. John stepped closer to the boulder and leaned over. George had taken a bullet square in the middle of the forehead.

"Mauser, I'm thinking," Edwards said. "He wouldn't of gave them so clear a shot if he still had cartridges."

"Wasn't a Mauser did that to his face. Not the business end anyway." The posse chief's voice was tight.

"I'm thinking they done that after he was dead. You can

see the boot prints by daylight. It was Merle done it.
There's a clear blood trail leading to where George had his
horse hobbled. Busted open his wound during the kicking.
That's how I read it.''

"Race with him?"

"Appears that way. They won't get far, both sitting that
little 'stang of George's.''

"Got all the time in the world, seeing as how no one's
chasing them.''

The words were barbed. Edwards reacted with a tragic
face. "It was coming on sundown when we got here,
Cap'n.''

St. John caught him on the point of his chin with a doubled fist and he went down. The sharpshooter's rifle cart-
wheeled out of his grasp. Dazed, then furious, Edwards
clawed at the Colt in his holster. He was still lying on the
ground. Something crunched and St. John's Peacemaker
hovered near his face. He relaxed.

"I said before you should of told me your problem at
the start,'' St. John said. "George didn't die because he ran
out of ammunition. He died because you were too blind to
come here with him, and the ones killed him are breathing
free air right now because you're too blind to follow. Give
me one good reason why I shouldn't put out the rest of
your lights right here.''

They watched each other, Edwards blankly, seeing nothing past his spectacles in the failing light. The wind buzzed
between rocks and lifted St. John's coattails. Behind him
Paco and Diego had reached the high ground and stood
watching quietly.

St. John replaced the hammer and put away the gun.
"Get a fire going. We pull out first light. First light, if you
got to grope your way into the saddle.'' He told the Mexicans in rapid Spanish to dig a hole for George.

Edwards stayed on the ground. "What about Shirley and
the woman?''

"Varmint meat. We'll turn in his Colt and rig for the
reward. I didn't think to pack the Pinkerton's camera or I'd
take their pictures,'' he added acidly.

"How is he?"

"Healthier than Testament. The psalm singer's dead."
He walked away without explaining.

They buried the Indian under a three-quarter moon and
covered the grave with rocks to keep the wolves and coyotes from scratching him up. Standing next to Edwards over
the mound, St. John took off his hat.

"He never did like the outdoors," he said. "He once
told me if it was a choice between the Happy Hunting
Ground and a seat in front of a furnace in hell, he'd take
hell. But injuns do what's expected of them."

"We're all serving some kind of sentence," put in Edwards.

They moved away, toward the fire. "I shouldn't of hit
you." St. John fished out his pipe and worn pouch. "Had
it to do again I wouldn't."

"He was my friend too."

"You read trail?"

Edwards smiled weakly in the light of the flames.
"About as well as I shoot at night."

"No matter. They'll be heading down the Outlaw Trail
to Brown's Hole. No other way for them to go."

"That's better'n two hundred miles. They'll be stopping
for fresh mounts first chance they get."

St. John set the tobacco burning with a stick from the
fire. "So will we. But at least we're not underhorsed. We'll
catch up before they make that first stop." Flipping away
the stick, he sat down on the ground puffing clouds of
smoke. "Or feed the buzzards trying."

They found Merle toward the close of the next day, when
a corner of brown corduroy coat caught their attention stirring in the breeze from behind a patch of scrub oak. His
face was like clear wax and he had begun to stiffen. His
left pantleg was crusted black from thigh to boot.

"Bled out," announced St. John. "Four, maybe six
hours ago from the feel of him."

"Damn decent of his own cousin to give him a Christian
burial." Edwards spat the words.

"No Christians on the scout."

The old lawman unbuttoned the dead man's coat, found a canvas money belt buckled around his middle and undid that. He opened one of the pouches and began pulling out crumpled bills. "Christ, there must be near ten thousand here."

"The others must of buried theirs."

Something metallic clicked. St. John turned around, a space ahead of Edwards. Paco and Diego grinned at them over their big Colts.

They argued over the gringos' fate. In the end it was caution that saved them. Robbed and left to themselves they were two saddle tramps, nothing more; dead they were martyrs, and white posses would hunt their killers to hell and back. Had not the governor of Texas unleashed *los rangeros* merely because a pair of Mexicans had dared to lay hands upon one of his fellow gringos?

They disarmed their prisoners, bound them, unloaded the confiscated weapons, and cast the cartridges and gun belts into the open spaces. They could do without the extra weight. Then they emptied the money belt and divided the bills equally, lastly taking what they needed from their victims' saddlebags and slapping away their horses before they rode on. They charted a southerly course toward Mexico.

Camping outside Trinidad, Colorado one week later, they broke out the last of the whiskey and played blackjack with Diego's frayed and faded pasteboards. The betting grew heavy as the fire burned low, and by midnight Paco was down to his last fifty dollars. He wagered it all on the last hand and lost it when Diego drew eighteen and he went bust. Paco shot his partner while he was raking in the ante. Diego's eyes went round and he fell face down on top of the money. Paco lifted his head by the hair to collect the bills, wiped the blood off them onto the dead grass, and went through his pockets for the rest. He slept the remainder of the night and left before dawn without bothering to bury or otherwise conceal the body.

More days passed. The Porfiristas were active when he

crossed into Mexico, searching the haciendas and haystacks for bandits. Paco hid in the attic of one of his many cousins to wait for the *federales* to move on before continuing to Chihuahua. Early on the second morning of his stay, he was dragged from his straw pallet by armed soldiers who marched him with a ragged and barefoot band of sleepy brigands to a bullet-chewed wall in the village square and ordered them to stand two feet apart. They were shot one at a time from right to left, the five rifles sounding in staggered volley like rocks bounding down a ravine. Paco was third. The first bullet tore through his lungs and knocked yellow dust out of the wall behind him. The second struck his thigh, smarting like a blow from a willow branch. He took the third in the chest and didn't feel the other two.

The government paid Paco's cousin two new pesos for delivering an enemy of the Republic.

St. John managed to work himself free, untie Edwards, and recover their guns and ammunition just as darkness set in and joined Edwards at the fire. The flames were strictly for warmth, as their provisions had gone the way of their horses and of the Mexicans, who were still heading south. With the cloud cover gone, a black, brittle cold crouched beyond the orange glow. The stars were ice crystals in a frozen sky.

"There's a big ranch about twelve miles west," Edwards volunteered. "Used to belong to a fellow named Harper. We can get us some mounts there tomorrow."

The old lawman said nothing. His nose was running and his joints hurt.

Edwards guessed the reason for his companion's silence. "It wasn't your fault, Cap'n. Man's only got two eyes."

"George and Rawlings both warned me about them." St. John's eyes were dark-rimmed. His face looked gray in the firelight. "I said I could handle them. That was Deputy Marshal Ike St. John talking. I clean forgot he was dead."

"Forget 'em. They'll get theirs. Ain't no such thing as a forty-year-old *bandido*. Merle there puts us three-quarters of the way to that twenty thousand the Pinkertons promised you.''

''The hell with the twenty thousand. I want Race.''

The fire crackled and burned blue. Edwards used a stick to trace a map in the earth, hunkered down so low to see what he was doing that the tip of his hat brim actually touched ground. Hole-in-the-Wall west to Thermopolis, then south through Riverton and Lander and Atlantic City and Rock Springs and past Flaming Gorge across the border into Colorado and Brown's Hole, then down through Colorado and New Mexico to El Paso and the Rio Grande with old Mexico beckoning from the other side.

''It ain't so bad as it looks,'' he told St. John. ''A heap of these places stopped being strongholds when the developers came and the outlaws' friends moved on. They got law till it slops over and makes puddles. A few telephone calls and it'll be like running game.''

''That's the way I want it.'' St. John stood up. ''Just like hunting an animal. Sleep fast. We got a hike in the morning.''

Judge Parker came to St. John that night, or rather St. John came to him, in his chambers outside the Fort Smith courtroom, with the portrait of President Cleveland on the wall above the judge's head. Parker sat behind the desk in his Prince Albert and vest with the gold chain hooked on the front. There was gray in his hair and chin whiskers. His eyes were heavy-lidded, set deep and sleepy-looking. They had led more than one ambitious young attorney into attempting to slip a questionable tactic past his straight, thick nose, only to receive a sharp lecture in American jurisprudence and a promise of a contempt citation if the incident was repeated.

''St. John, isn't it?'' The soft baritone rode the air in the large room a moment after he had finished speaking.

''Yes, sir.''

''How long has it been since we've talked?''

St. John considered. He fought the urge to turn his hat brim around and around in his hands, as he used to do when his father was preparing to reprimand him for some child-hood transgression. "Ten years, I reckon," he ventured. "It's been that long since you—" He stopped, mortified.

"Died." Parker was annoyed. "Use the word, man. You know how I feel about euphemisms in my court. Yes, I've been dead ten years. And what have you been doing mean-while?"

Hesitantly the old lawman told him, glossing over his marriage and business failures and lingering on his quest for public office, thinking the old federal appointee would be interested in that part of his life. But Parker cut him off with an impatient gesture.

"I don't want to hear about Congress. Didn't I hear enough from them when they were whittling away at my jurisdiction? What are you doing now?"

"Looking for a fellow named Buckner."

"Why?"

"He robbed some banks and trains. And his cousin killed George American Horse."

"Oh, yes, the Crow tracker. I remember when he testified in the Blackfeather trial. He was your friend, wasn't he?" He read the answer in St. John's eyes. "Well, this sort of thing won't do. You know my policy on personal vendettas. Let someone else take charge of the manhunt."

St. John was embarrassed. "Beg pardon, your honor, but this isn't your honor's case."

Parker gave him a look that would melt stone. Then his face relaxed by degrees, as from an effort of will. He sat back in the armchair. "We're cut from the same bolt, you and I," he said calmly. "We both place justice ahead of everything, including the law. That's why the Congress shoved me aside, and it's why there's no more place for you on the frontier." He paused. "I've saved you a seat in the gallery, Swami Ike."

"I—I don't follow you, sir."

"Oh, but you will." Parker smiled faintly behind his hand, as he used to do during light moments in court. "That will be all, St. John. We'll talk again soon."

•   •   •

He awoke in darkness with a great weight on his chest. He tried to fill his lungs and failed. His heart thudded irregularly in his ears. He sought to take his mind off his discomfort by pondering his dream, but the details were already fading. He felt nauseated. His left arm had fallen asleep. Awakening, it tingled. Worst of all was his inability to get enough air. Then he remembered Judge Parker's last words, and when the real pain came it found him in the gallery of the courtroom in Fort Smith.

At first light Wild Bill Edwards tried to awaken him, recoiling when his hands touched the cold stiffness under the blanket.

THIRTY-ONE

The Border

Through the window of his ground-floor quarters in the El Paso rooming house, Race glowered at the guards on the bridge leading across the Rio Grande into Mexico and waited for darkness. The room was a reconditioned pantry with a side door leading into the kitchen and through it to freedom outside if someone he didn't want to see came to the front. He had a bed and a washstand, and it was all costing him only a thousand dollars a day. His face was on every wall and post for a dozen blocks.

He made himself as comfortable as possible on his back in the hollow of the mattress and contemplated the cracks in the ceiling, thinking of Jim Shirley. He missed the cripple more than he missed Merle, with whom he had never really gotten along and whom he had more than once considered cutting from the gang because of his constant grousing over the conditions of life on the scout. Shirley's quiet strength had been a thing to rely on in emergencies, and Race had liked him besides. The Indian woman was already a shadow, as easily forgotten in death as she was in life.

Too late, the fugitive had discovered that outlaw income was directly related to the cost of being wanted, that the things ordinary citizens took for granted came at a premium when one was forced to depend on less conspicuous channels. The seven thousand dollars left in his possession would buy him a week's lodging at the going rate. He knew now that the stories of the James gang's buried wealth were just stories; the shovel alone would have cost them at least five hundred.

Merle had been right about one thing: there would be no quitting. Though Mexico beckoned, it was too poor a country to support a man, and there was only one occupation on this side of the border that would keep food in his stomach. He would need help, of course. El Paso was full of talent. In four or five months, when his heels stopped burning, he'd come back across the river to recruit.

He paid the sour-faced landlady fifty dollars for a fresh newspaper and spread it out on the floor to read, the way he had done since childhood. His eyes fixed on the item headed FAMED LAWMAN DEAD. The black-bordered piece was brief, drawing most of its material from newspaper accounts of Irons St. John's adventures in the Nations. Little of his early life was public knowledge. The writer mentioned St. John's recent bid for Congress and ended with the various rumors surrounding his activities at the time of his death.

Race Buckner stopped reading and sat back on his heels. "So that's who it was," he muttered.

THIRTY-TWO

Going Home

B lowing snow rattled against the depot wall in Cheyenne and stung like hot sparks wherever it found exposed flesh. It hissed against the wheezing boiler, running down in rivulets to join the condensed moisture dripping off the end of the steam jets. The drifting clouds of vapor felt like expelled breath and smelled like wet wool drying next to a stove.

Emmett Force Rawlings was waiting on the platform when Wild Bill Edwards stepped down from the last car and hailed him. The Pinkerton's face brightened. It was a trifle pale, and the hollows in his cheeks together with his beard gave him the look of an early martyr. His checked suit and overcoat hung on his frame. He waited for the sharpshooter to join him.

Edwards set down his traps and gently accepted the gloved hand that was gingerly offered him. The detective's grip was steady, though a tad weak. "How you feeling?"

"Like a horse kicked me," said Rawlings. "Dr. Urquhart screamed bloody murder when I said I was leaving. I think he was planning to publish a paper on my case. But an anvil couldn't have held me to that cot after I read your wire.'' He breathed some of the steam-sodden air. ''Where is he?''

''In a box in the baggage car. I had to use some of that advance the Cap'n gave me in Kansas City to get him on this run. W. R. Hearst's aboard in a private car and I'm told he don't much hold with dead ones sharing his train.''

A porter picked up Rawlings' bag and carried it on board. Said the Pinkerton: ''I wired his widow in Rock Springs. She's taking care of the funeral arrangements there. Will you be coming with me the rest of the way?''

Edwards shook his head. ''What about Race Buckner?''

''The agency has authorized me to gather a new posse and follow him into Mexico if necessary. The legal papers will be waiting for us in El Paso when we reach the border. I'd like to include you,'' he added.

''No, you wouldn't. I'd be Race's best friend in your camp. If I thought otherwise I'd of went on chasing him after the Cap'n—'' He shrugged.

''I've always been curious about that. Why did you call him 'Captain'?''

Edwards blinked rapidly behind his spectacles. ''Because that's what he was.''

Rawlings didn't pursue the point. ''He was a hard man to understand,'' he said, glancing toward the windowless baggage car.

''Not to me.''

''The agency will make good on its offer of a thousand dollars for each of the gang members killed.'' The Pinkerton was changing the subject. ''They didn't want to agree to St. John's wages of two hundred per week, but I burned up the wires between Denver and Cheyenne until they gave in. I can't accept any of the reward, so half of it goes to you. St. John's widow gets the rest. Neither George nor Pierce left heirs.''

''Send me a draft care of the Brevoort Hotel in New York City. I stayed there once with Comanche Tom's show. I reckon they'll hold it for me. My gratuities run high when I'm flush,'' Edwards explained.

''What will you do in New York City?''

"Well, I'll be spending most of my time across the river in New Jersey, try to get into moving pictures. They'll be needing sharpshooters in them Westerns. I got two, maybe three good years left and I reckon they'll put them to good use."

Rawlings made no comment. They both knew the chances of a man who wore eyeglasses making a success on the screen. "You won't reconsider and come with me?"

Again Edwards shook his head. "But I can give you some names." He recited some, providing general locations where he could, while the Pinkerton scribbled in his pocket pad. Edwards hesitated before concluding, "I got to say some of them have done time behind bars."

"I hardly thought otherwise."

The train whistle blew. Rawlings put away the pad and extended his hand, smiling sadly. "Good luck."

Edwards grasped it. "You too, Cap'n."